THE TRIAL OF
PRISONER 043

TERRY JASTROW

FOUR SPRINGS PRESS

Four Springs Press
501 S. Beverly Drive, 3rd Floor
Beverly Hills, CA 90212
www.fourspringspress.com

Publisher's Note: This story is set in the future. It is a product of the author's imagination. The courtroom testimony and other comments are based on real statements by real people involved in historical events, but the novel itself is a work of fiction. Real places or institutions are used novelistically, and no affiliation or endorsement by such places or institutions is claimed or implied.

Ordering Information

Quantity sales. Special discounts are available on quantity purchases by corporations, associations, and others. For details, contact the "Special Sales Department" at the address above.

Order by US trade bookstores and wholesalers. Please contact BCH: (800) 431-1579 or visit http://www.bookch.com/ for details.

Printed in the United States of America

Cataloging-in-Publication Data

Jastrow, Terry, author.
   The trial of prisoner 043 / Terry Jastrow. -- First edition.
   pages cm
   Includes bibliographical references.
   LCCN 2017939403
   ISBN 978-1-946241-14-6 (hdcv)
   ISBN 978-1-946241-15-3 (pb)
   ISBN 978-1-946241-16-0 (ebook)

1. Bush, George W. (George Walker), 1946---Trials, litigation, etc.--Fiction. 2. International Criminal Court--Fiction. 3. War crime trials--Fiction. 4. Iraq War, 2003-2011--Atrocities-- Fiction. 5. Legal fiction (Literature) I. Title.

   PS3610.A88T75 2017   813'.6
   QBI17-757

First Edition

21 20 19 18 17   10 9 8 7 6 5 4 3 2 1

To those who lost their lives or
were wounded in George W. Bush's war,
in the sincere hope their death or injury
was not in vain.

Table of Contents

CHAPTER ONE   The Abduction   1

CHAPTER TWO   Feeding Frenzy   13

CHAPTER THREE   Setting the Table   17

CHAPTER FOUR   Welcome to the International Criminal Court   23

CHAPTER FIVE   The Cavalry Arrives   35

CHAPTER SIX   Facing the Music   41

CHAPTER SEVEN   Resumption   59

CHAPTER EIGHT   Eye of the Storm   75

CHAPTER NINE   Dueling Barristers   81

CHAPTER TEN   Parade of Prosecution Witnesses   91

CHAPTER ELEVEN   Heavy Artillery   115

CHAPTER TWELVE   Quid Pro Quo   131

CHAPTER THIRTEEN   Family Matters   149

CHAPTER FOURTEEN   In Search of the Truth   157

CHAPTER FIFTEEN   Practice What You Preach   185

CHAPTER SIXTEEN   Back in the Saddle   191

CHAPTER SEVENTEEN   A Winter's Nightmare   205

CHAPTER EIGHTEEN   The Tale of Two Trials   211

CHAPTER NINETEEN   Final Arguments   215

CHAPTER TWENTY   Can There Be Justice?   227

CHAPTER TWENTY-ONE   All Over but the Shouting   235

Author's Notes   239

Acknowledgments   245

About the Author   247

CHAPTER ONE

The Abduction

The play's the thing wherein
I'll catch the conscience of the king.
—William Shakespeare

Early on a glorious September morning in St. Andrews, Scotland, former president of the United States George W. Bush approached the first tee of the world's most famous golf course to play a round of golf he would not finish.

Assembled around the first tee were a few hundred local residents and a handful of members of the Royal & Ancient Golf Club. Known simply as the "R&A," the club is the governing body and custodian of the rules for all golfing countries except the United States, which has its own governing body. The occasion was the annual driving-in ceremony of the newly elected captain of the R&A. Mr. Bush arrived at the first tee, scanned the Old Course, which had been the site of many historic championships, and began to mingle with the members.

Precisely at eight o'clock, the retiring captain preceded the new captain as they marched out of the R&A Clubhouse, down the ancient stone steps, and onto the first tee. In typically understated R&A fashion, nothing was said. The new captain took a few modest warm-up swings, addressed the ball, and hit a lovely tee shot down the middle of the fairway.

BOOM. At the precise moment of contact, an ancient cannon situated off the first tee was fired to mark the occasion. A few dozen local caddies scattered about the fairway scrambled for the ball as it careened down the fairway, until the winning caddie scooped it up, raised it over his head triumphantly to the jeering of his peers, and proudly strutted up to the first tee.

When the caddie arrived, the captain shook his hand in congratulations and, as was the custom, gave him a gold sovereign coin worth about two hundred pounds.

If it sounds unusual, it is. No other club has such a ceremony, and it has occurred in exactly the same way since 1863, when the Prince of Wales, later King Edward VII, "drove in" as captain.

The tee times following the driving-in ceremony are traditionally reserved for former prime ministers, presidents, or other visiting dignitaries. And so it was on this occasion that George W. Bush and two club members stepped onto the first tee and were greeted by R&A secretary Harold Maxwell. "Gentlemen. Mr. President. Good day to you all."

"It'll be a good day," Bush said, shaking hands, "if I don't make a fool of myself by chunking it into the Swilcan Burn on the first hole, or yanking it into the Road Bunker at seventeen."

"I'm sure you'll do just fine."

"You're more sure than I am."

Secretary Maxwell chuckled. "We were very pleased to welcome your father here as a new member after he finished his presidency."

"Yeah, he loved golf and he loved St. Andrews, that's for sure."

"There's a little-known story about your father that says a lot about him as a man. In December of the year he played his first round at the Old Course, he sent his caddie a handwritten letter thanking him for making his experience in St. Andrews so special and wishing him a Merry Christmas. I do believe that was a first."

"He must've been a good caddie."

"Must have been."

"Guessing you fellows don't allow mulligans," Bush said, looking out at the fairway.

"No mulligans, but we can offer a swallow of scotch if that will settle your nerves?"

"Not my nerves I got a problem with. It's my damn golf swing. Forsakes me every time when I need it the most . . . like now!"

The secretary commented, "That's just about the widest fairway in the world, so it shouldn't present much of a problem. Enjoy."

It would be fair to say every golfer in the world dreams of playing the Old Course at St. Andrews. Bush approached the ball, took his stance, and then *nervously* jerked the club away and swung. Mercifully, the ball curved only slightly to the right and came to rest in the fairway.

Bush smiled mischievously. "Not bad for a broken-down ol' president. What's the course record around here anyway?"

"In the Open Championship . . . sixty-three."

"Sixty-three, hell! I will've hit it that many times by the twelfth hole," Bush said as he winked at the secretary and stepped aside to allow his playing partners their turn.

From a position three hundred yards away on a public footpath that bordered the fairway, a middle-aged man of generic features lowered his binoculars and turned to saunter away, whistling as he went. As he reached up to scratch his nose, he spoke quietly into a microphone buried inside the sleeve of his sweater. "Blue sweater, white shirt, gray pants, black shoes, no hat."

In a secluded wooded area two kilometers from the golf course, a nondescript brown van and midsize blue car were parked side by side. Huddled inside the van were eight British paramilitary commandos. Sitting inside the car were four more commandos. Six of the twelve were carrying assorted weaponry. Hearing the description of Bush's wardrobe, the driver of the van keyed his radio and answered in a noticeably British accent, "Copy that. Cowboy Justice a go." The drivers of the van and the car exchanged informal salutes, started their vehicles, and sped away.

Poised with engines running on the edge of a runway at the Rotterdam Airport, pilots strapped inside the cockpits of a Hawker 800XP and Learjet 85 received the same message and answered back in turn: "Cowboy Justice a go. Hawker 1 copy."

"Learjet 1, copy that as well."

The Hawker took off in an angry roar, followed quickly by the Learjet.

The most famous hole on the Old Course at St. Andrews is the seventeenth, commonly referred to as the Road Hole. The green sits hard by a cobblestone road, on the other side of which is a stone wall that for centuries has presented unusual and difficult challenges for golfers.

George Bush, midway through a Cuban cigar, and his caddie, Oliver Croft, stepped onto the seventeenth tee along with his playing partners and their caddies. Bush tossed his cigar to the ground and considered his options as Oliver offered a word of encouragement. "Nice and easy does it, sir."

"Nice and easy? Not my strong suit," Bush said before pushing his tee shot into the right rough. "More or less like Jack Nicklaus did it."

"More 'less' than 'more,' I'm afraid, sir," Oliver responded.

Bush picked up his cigar and headed down the fairway, saying, "Let's go see if we can birdie this bad boy."

As Bush made his way along the seventeenth fairway, the brown van and blue car pulled into the parking lot of the Jigger Inn, a famous St. Andrews watering hole located short and to the right of the seventeenth green.

Just as Bush arrived at his ball, the twelve British commandos poured out of their vehicles and precisely according to a well-crafted and rehearsed plan, sprinted straight for the former president, his playing partners, and their caddies.

Immediately realizing what was happening, Bush turned and ran for his life. The much faster commandos quickly tackled him to the ground. With the former president lying facedown on the turf, one commando lifted his head back allowing a second commando to put a cloth soaked with diethyl ether over his mouth and nose to both mute and anesthetize him. Two other commandos strapped a leather belt around his ankles, slapped handcuffs on his wrists, and slipped a hood over his head. Once Bush was unconscious, gagged, shackled, cuffed, and hooded, the commandos carefully lifted him and carried him away.

Simultaneously and similarly, five commandos contained Bush's caddie, his playing partners, and their caddies.

Immediately upon seeing the attack, three distinctly American-looking men dressed in Scottish golf attire rushed to Bush's aid. Expecting Secret Service protection for the former president, the remaining commandos fired stun guns at the oncoming agents, who, one by one, stumbled and fell to the ground.

The commandos carrying Bush placed him in the back of the van and fled.

The entire series of events took less than six minutes and occurred with little commotion and hardly any noise. The stealth abduction of a former president of the United States from the world's most famous golf course—against his will, in broad daylight—was a stark contrast to the peace and grandeur of this ancient town, the resting ground of Saint Andrew the Apostle.

Eventually, a few passing townspeople noticed the bound bodies strewn over the seventeenth fairway and rushed to help. Once Bush's playing partners and the caddies were untethered, the lot of them raced up the eighteenth fairway waving their arms and yelling hysterically, "Help! Help!" "They abducted the president!" "Help, please, for the love of God!"

Located six miles from St. Andrews was the hamlet of Leuchars, famous for its RAF airfield. The Hawker and Learjet landed and sped to their appointed destination. With clockwork precision, the van carrying Bush pulled up alongside the Learjet. The commandos transferred his now conscious but still restrained body onto the plane.

Other commandos entered the Hawker's passenger cabin. Not by happenstance, another man who looked remarkably like George Bush—about the same age, hair color, height, weight, and facial features, and wearing the same clothes— joined the team. The commandos sat the Bush look-alike in a window seat, thus creating a Bush decoy. The commandos deplaned and scattered. Immediately the Hawker screamed down the runway and lifted off, heading west to Glasgow.

The Learjet carrying Bush took off in a southeasterly direction. Destination unknown.

Inside the R&A Clubhouse, the secretary was on the phone with Scotland Yard explaining what had happened as best he could. Behind the eighteenth green of the Old Course, Scottish police were questioning Bush's playing partners and the caddies. What they knew would fill a thimble. What they didn't know would fill a novel.

Two RAF jets flew up to and alongside each side of the Hawker. The pilots spotted the Bush decoy, radioed they had found the former president, and requested a convoy of military aircraft to help escort the Hawker to Glasgow.

Meanwhile, the Learjet carrying Bush flew close to the ground to avoid conventional radar. Aboard, the commandos removed the hood, gag, shackles, and handcuffs from Bush who immediately asked, "Who the hell are you guys?"

"You will know soon enough," the attending commando coldly responded. "You do not need to worry. You will not be harmed."

"You're British, aren't you?"

"Yes."

"What the fuck are you doing?" Bush erupted in anger. "You're supposed to be our ally."

The commando shot back, "No, Tony Blair is your ally. Most British people hated your war."

The Learjet landed at its appointed destination, the Rotterdam Airport, and taxied to a stop next to a waiting chopper, rotary blades spinning. United Nations police quickly and silently escorted Bush off the jet and into the chopper, which took off immediately.

Boxed in by four escort jets flying in close formation, the Hawker landed at Glasgow Airport and taxied to a stop. Police cars and vans quickly pulled up to create a 360-degree barricade. Two dozen Scottish police officers under the command of Chief Constable Angus Duff drew their weapons and aimed at the plane. Government officials positioned themselves behind the police cars.

The Hawker door opened. The pilot descended the stairs, protesting, "What the hell is going on here?"

Over a megaphone from behind the barricade, Duff responded, "You know. Where is he?"

"Where is who?"

"Deliver him unharmed or you will be spending the rest of your life in a cold dark box from which you will never emerge."

The pilot dug in his heels. "Are you out of your mind? Your jets flew dangerously close to our aircraft in blatant violation of international flight regulations. And now you're falsely accusing us of having some mythical passenger onboard."

Without responding, Constable Duff signaled a dozen Scottish police wearing body armor and carrying machine guns to board and search the plane.

A peaceful silence at The Hague was broken by the sound of helicopter blades whirring as a chopper approached a make-shift landing pad between the International Criminal Court and the ICC Detention Centre, situated two and a half kilometers apart. The chopper landed gently, its blades continuing to rotate as four security guards approached the door and politely but firmly escorted Bush off the chopper. No words were spoken. They swiftly led him through a back door into the detention center. The chopper sped away, mission accomplished.

The reception area of the detention center is small but functional, its walls bare except for a simple portrait of the UN secretary-general. The guards escorted Bush to a single chair in front of the desk where sat a Kenyan guard, Mobwana Mochellus. "Hello, Mr. Bush. Welcome to the Detention Centre of the International Criminal Court."

Bush did not respond. Mochellus continued. "Consistent with ICC protocol, I will inform you of your living quarters for the foreseeable future. Each detainee is assigned a private cell that includes a single bed, desk, chair, bookshelves, toilet, hand basin, television, and computer. We provide three meals a day, but detainees also have access to a communal kitchen if they wish to cook for themselves.

"The ICC provides a variety of recreational opportunities at selected times, including walks in the courtyard, a basketball court, and an exercise gym. You can also elect to partake in manual activities such as gardening, painting—we hear you like to paint, so that might be of interest—woodcrafts, and other such activities. You will receive medical and dental care as and when needed. Detainees can have visitors at prearranged times, and certain phone calls are permitted. However, you should know that phone calls as well as computer usage will be monitored."

With her speech successfully delivered, Mochellus reached into a closet and brought out a bundle of clothes. "Here are your ICC prison clothes and pajamas. We guessed your size. Let us know if you need anything else. It's not required for detainees to wear prison clothes in court, so we procured a few dark suits we thought you might want to wear. Do you have any questions, Mr. Bush?"

"Yes," he answered. "Is there a Bible in the room?"

"I'll make sure there is."

Orientation completed, the prison guards escorted an angry and tired former president George W. Bush, carrying his prison garb, out of the reception area.

The events of the day sent America's top political, legal, and military authorities into a tailspin. Not since the September 11 attacks had so many high-powered meetings been so hastily assembled to discuss such a daunting crisis of international importance. The day culminated in a late-night meeting at the Pentagon of the president's senior advisors, including Secretary of Defense John Cox and the Joint Chiefs of Staff.

Secretary Cox began, "Gentlemen, the president asked for recommendations within the hour on how the hell we can rescue George W. Bush from the ICC."

"If the bastards think they can just nab the president of the United States and get away with it," barked Army general Arthur Lexton, "they got another *think* coming."

"*Former* president," corrected Admiral Dick Dohring.

Marine commandant Stephen Wells interjected, "Same thing. If they can arbitrarily kidnap a former president, they can grab any of our top government officials. We need to let them know we're not going to stand for this horseshit."

General William Shackelford addressed Secretary Cox. "Sir, we have several scenarios in play that are ready to engage."

"Such as?"

"Option one is the insertion of SEALs from Task Force 64, Special Ops assigned to the Sixth Fleet, headquartered in Naples. They can fly over the Swiss Alps and be on the ground in The Hague by twenty-three hundred hours GMT. Minimal collateral damage expected.

"Option two is a standard amphibious assault. The ICC Detention Centre is situated on the banks of the North Sea, easily accessible by Marine forces. The Dutch would not contest a rescue attempt as their defenses in that area are light and they will not be expecting an amphibious invasion. We currently have assets returning from the Arctic that could carry out this mission ASAP. Again, minimal collateral damage expected.

"Option three is a stealth Delta Force chopper landing under cover of night. Special Ops Forces would breach the detention center and extract the former president. This option utilizes forces and air assets stationed in Germany. A larger degree of collateral damage is to be expected with this option."

"Thank you, General," Secretary Cox said, nodding. "Well conceived."

"Sir, I understand this is an awful situation and sets a bad precedent," Admiral Dohring added, "but if we recommend to the president that we invade the Netherlands, we're recommending military aggression that will violate its sovereignty and be in contradiction of the UN Charter."

General Lexton scoffed. "Too damn bad. We didn't care much about violating the UN Charter when we kicked Saddam's ass out of Kuwait."

"Let's not forget, gentlemen," Cox cautioned, "that the Dutch are our allies. They didn't kidnap George Bush. It was a private security firm arranged by some of our British *friends*. The Dutch have fought alongside us since World War II. We're both members of NATO and, according to Article 5 of the NATO treaty, if one of its members is attacked, the other members must regard it as an attack against all. Britain, France, Spain, Germany, even Canada, are all bound by the treaty to respond."

Admiral Dohring countered, "So you're saying if we send a stealth rescue squad to The Hague, it would be considered an attack on the Netherlands and trigger a violation of the NATO treaty?"

"Possibly, yes," responded Shackelford. "Do we really want to risk a counterattack on our homeland by forces from Canada, for God's sake? They would have every legal right to do so under the NATO treaty."

Wells shook his head. "Shit, that's crazy. Unthinkable."

"The whole thing is crazy," Cox added. "Thank you, gentlemen. There are a myriad of global issues in play here that the president needs to be aware of. I'm choppering over to the White House now to discuss our options. Keep your powder dry, gentlemen."

In the ICC Detention Centre, George Bush, wearing prison pajamas, sat slumped on the edge of the bed in his cell, six meters long and three meters wide, reliving the events of the day, wondering what was going to happen tomorrow, and perhaps even mildly chastising himself for venturing over to Scotland to play golf and not bothering to pay more attention to the ICC.

CHAPTER TWO

Feeding Frenzy

*Paramount among the responsibilities of a free press
is the duty to prevent any part of the government from
deceiving the people and sending them off to distant
lands to die of . . . foreign shot and shell.*
—Hugo Black, US Supreme Court Justice, 1937–71

The word "news" means "previously unknown information having a specified influence or effect." Usually, however, TV news gathering and reporting saturates the airwaves with the daily drip, drip, drip of fires, floods, shootings, stabbings, robberies, rapes, muggings, murders, divorces, deaths, etcetera.

Once in a great while an event transcends "news" and becomes culturally relevant. It could be a man walking on the moon, a black woman riding on a bus in the South, a royal birth or wedding, the assassination of a world leader, or the abduction of a former president of the United States.

In the United States, as lunchtime transitioned into mid-afternoon, Americans first began to hear about this near unimaginable story. The events in St. Andrews were newsworthy by anybody's definition, and the biggest and best news organizations were in an all-hands-on-deck, man-the-battle-stations frenzy. America's most respected broadcasters canceled whatever programming was scheduled to allow for nonstop reporting of the one story everybody cared about. Not only would ratings spike to all-time heights, but awards for outstanding news reporting would be on the line, and nobody in the news business wanted to miss this once-in-a-lifetime chance at greatness. CNN engaged its considerable forces to provide comprehensive coverage. Major networks reassigned resources and repurposed facilities to stay astride of the fast-breaking story.

CBS's Kenneth McLane began, "We've just learned that only a few hours ago former president of the United States George W. Bush was abducted while playing golf in St. Andrews, Scotland. At approximately eleven forty-five a.m. GMT, Mr. Bush was carried off the course by an unidentified group of assailants and taken to a destination as yet unknown."

Duncan Evans on ABC reported, "It is a known fact that Mr. Bush doesn't travel outside the United States much, as he is thought to be in some legal jeopardy over the waging of the Iraq War. But any speculation in that regard would be just that, speculation."

William Huff on NBC stated, "Indications are that Mr. Bush did have the standard allotment of Secret Service agents on site, but obviously they did not provide the requisite protection for the former president."

Sarah Clossey on Fox concluded, "Mr. Bush's playing partners were not harmed and are reportedly cooperating with law enforcement authorities. So we can only deduce that former president Bush was specifically targeted for the abduction. No doubt the perpetrators, whoever they are, will pay a hefty price for this crime of the highest order."

The main question most Americans were asking was, "Where in the world is George W. Bush?" The recent flurry of activity in

The Hague, coupled with a few strategic leaks from keen ICC observers, began to inform people of the answer. He had been taken against his will to the International Criminal Court— wherever that was.

Dark clouds gathered over the magnificent new headquarters of the International Criminal Court, providing an ominous clue of what was about to come. The design of the ICC building was intended to reflect the transparency of the institution itself. The complex consists of six buildings sided with colorfully arranged geometric squares. A moat encompasses the buildings, featuring concrete walkways that connect the buildings on the ground floor.

The following morning, elite press from around the world began to arrive in anticipation of the upcoming case, which promised to be of huge international interest. The people of the press were in a giddy mood, suggesting hyenas circling for a kill. First to arrive and start setting up were British teams from the BBC, Sky TV, and ITV. Not long after, news agencies from the United States arrived, followed quickly by networks from around the globe, including, notably, Iraq. Eventually thirty or so of the world's elite news companies arrived, with an air of anticipation similar to that surrounding the Olympic Games, the coronation of a monarch, or the FIFA World Cup finals.

The ICC press team was well prepared to handle visiting press; nonetheless, the herd of producers, directors, camera crews, and reporters from around the world created a stampede-like atmosphere. While most tried their best to be accommodating, nerves quickly became frazzled and egos got stomped. Nonetheless, the ICC press team doggedly assigned facilities such that each broadcaster would have a location to park its mobile unit and to set up production offices, and have a specifically assigned on-camera position at which its host announcers could be framed with the magnificent ICC building in the background.

The honor of doing the first on-the-scene live report of a breaking story is always the big prize among broadcasters. On this occasion it went to the BBC.

Standing, microphone in hand, dressed in a smart outfit, and possessing an air of authority, a multiple-award-winning news reporter began, "This is Elizabeth Reynolds reporting from the ICC at The Hague, where late yesterday the former president of the United States, George W. Bush, was brought to face charges for crimes we can only assume are in connection with the Iraq War. Many questions abound. Can the ICC do this legally under international law? Who specifically is responsible for this act of monumental arrogance and what will be the consequences? How quickly will the United States respond? Because most assuredly they will. Stay tuned for continuing coverage."

CHAPTER THREE

Setting the Table

He that is without sin,
let him cast the first stone.
—John 8:7

The International Criminal Court has eighteen judges in residence. As the Bush case was going to trial, the geographical breakdown of judges was five from Western Europe, four from Africa, three from Asia, three from Eastern Europe, and three from Latin America and the Caribbean. Of the eighteen ICC judges, six were women.

As there are no juries in international law, each case is assigned either one or three judges and verdicts are rendered accordingly—by the vote of one judge, or the majority vote of three judges. In the trial of *The Prosecutor v. George W. Bush*, three judges were assigned.

Once assigned to a case, the judges work to resolve all procedural matters leading up to the trial—most especially to oversee the Office of the Prosecutor (OTP) as it carries out its duties to guarantee the rights of suspects, victims, and witnesses in a fair and honest trial. The person who oversees the OTP is the chief prosecutor, whose principal function is to assign prosecuting attorneys most suited for the case. It was not of much surprise that the attorney selected to lead the prosecution in the case against George W. Bush was a hard-charging lawyer with top-of-the-class intelligence and an infectious smile, Michael David McBride.

Michael McBride was born forty-four years earlier in Denver, Colorado, to parents who were also litigators. Michael's mother specialized in child endangerment, prostitution, and abandonment cases. Michael's father's beat was corporate law, specifically focusing on corrupt banking. Michael was an outstanding high school basketball player and honors student, became a Rhodes scholar, attended Oxford in England, and returned to the United States to graduate with honors from Harvard Law School.

While at Oxford, Michael fell in love with the British culture, its refined use of language, and the hyperdiversity of its people. After graduating from Harvard Law, he moved back to London and immediately set up a private practice specializing in international criminal law. Concurrently, he reconnected with a former girlfriend at Oxford, Cheryl Stapleford, and soon thereafter they were married. Mrs. Stapleford-McBride was an accomplished art historian specializing in nineteenth-century Impressionists—Monet, Manet, Degas—the usual suspects. Eventually, theirs became a modern-day marriage of convenience. When the ICC recruited Michael to be the lead prosecuting attorney, he quickly packed his bags and moved to The Hague.

Michael was selected for the Bush case specifically *because* he was an American. To have a German or an Italian prosecuting a former US president would play into a defense argument regarding the legitimacy of the Court and the audacity of sitting in judgment of decisions made by an American president.

Co–prosecuting attorney Nadia Shadid, in her late thirties, came from an entirely different world. She was born and raised in Fallujah, Iraq, to a father who was a schoolteacher and a mother who was well known in the community as a leader in establishing Muslim women's rights. Although Nadia's family was Sunni, she grew up with a wide range of Shiite, Kurdish, Christian, and other nonsectarian friends.

While studying law at the University of Baghdad, she dated a fellow student who worked at night as the drummer in a local band. According to friends who knew them well, their dreams of happiness and success took divergent paths when Nadia discovered she was happier alone than with a man she could not totally love.

During her youth, Nadia's family lived next door to one of Iraq's most respected attorneys, who specialized in international law. He invited Nadia to join his prestigious London firm, Alliss, Blankenship & Coe. After six formative years during which she worked in the international litigation division, Nadia applied for and got an entry position in the Office of the Prosecutor at the International Criminal Court in The Hague.

Nadia and Michael had worked together on several cases, and it didn't take long for them to develop a mutual admiration and fondness. They were two very different people from very different worlds who found a common passion in international criminal law. Now they bore the honor and burden of prosecuting the case against a former president of the United States.

In fact, they were informed about the case a full twelve months before Bush's abduction. In a secure meeting deep in the bowels of the ICC building, the chief prosecuting attorney hinted that a case against Bush in connection with the Iraq War was in the works. Secretly they began to research all information available that, when considered as a whole, would constitute the legal precedent for a case against George Bush.

Late in the afternoon of a long day of preparation, and knowing full well their lives would be consumed by the trial for many weeks, months, or perhaps even years to come, Michael and Nadia went for an afternoon walk in a park near the ICC. Along the way Michael challenged Nadia: "It would be useful to understand the point of view of the Iraqi people about the war in order to prosecute this case effectively."

She didn't hesitate. "My people are conflicted. How one thinks of things is determined by one's religious affiliation: Sunni, Shiite, Kurd, Christian, whatever. If you are Sunni, as Saddam was, you might be upset that American and coalition forces removed him from power. If you are Shiite, Kurd, or one of the others, you're probably very happy not to live under his rule."

Michael pressed further. "One would think it would be a simple question of the common good for the greatest number of Iraqi citizens. Sooner or later, it would seem, there needs to be a common ground of understanding that the majority of Iraqi people could agree upon for the safety and security of all."

"Spoken like a true Westerner. The fundamental differences can be traced back thousands of years. They are not simple or easy to overcome."

"I understand, but take America. There are significant differences in the culture—rich/poor, religious/atheist, black/white, Democrat/Republican—but in desperate times Americans pull together as Americans. They seem to put their differences aside with the understanding that they are ultimately stronger together than divided. Look at Vietnam. There were once very significant differences between North and South. But today the Vietnamese people live and function together—and are stronger, safer, and happier for it. On the other hand there's North and South Korea. They remain opposed—each the greatest enemy of the other. As a result they continue to suffer the consequences of lack of cooperation."

"A theoretical deduction you might have a hard time convincing Koreans."

"Maybe so." Not wishing to dwell any longer, Michael pivoted to another question. "Do you think the majority of Iraqis are happy we're bringing Bush to trial?"

"Some are, not all. I think the majority of Iraqis opposed the war and will be happy to have justice served on those who caused it—starting with George Bush."

Michael thought it best to provide some perspective. "Do you know he didn't receive the majority of votes in his presidential election against Al Gore in 2000?"

Nadia raised her eyebrows. "He didn't?"

"No. He won with something in American politics called the 'electoral college' after a highly contentious recount in the state where his brother Jeb was governor—Florida. He got five hundred and forty-something thousand *fewer* votes than Gore."

"Similar to Hillary Clinton getting nearly three million more votes than Trump in 2016?"

"Correct."

As the earth turned away from the sun, leaving a magnificent sky of pinks and purples, Michael and Nadia paused to take in the grandeur of the western sky. After a moment of quiet reflection, Nadia said in a voice barely loud enough to hear, "If we don't win this case after what he did to my people, I will take a long walk into that sea."

Michael was surprised and touched. He moved in front of Nadia to confront her head-on. "I understand, but it's not considered best practice for prosecuting attorneys to let their personal passion interfere with the administration of justice."

She paused for a moment before speaking. "Michael, can I share something with you—and ask that it be kept confidential, just between us?"

"Sure."

"My cousin, my father's brother's oldest son, was killed three days into that war—in a firefight with American soldiers in Baghdad. His name was Jamali. He was my favorite cousin and closest friend." Nadia looked away to collect herself and continued slowly, "Sometimes, at night when I'm alone with my thoughts, I think about him because I hate how cruel war is to those who are made to fight."

CHAPTER FOUR

Welcome to the International Criminal Court

*No man is above the law . . . nor do we ask any man's
permission when we require him to obey it.*
—Theodore Roosevelt

All the principal characters were assembling inside the ICC courtroom to which the case of *The Prosecutor v. George W. Bush* had been assigned. The room was rectangular in shape, about twenty-five paces long and fifteen paces wide, adorned with beige wood paneling, and presenting itself as an ultramodern, highest-of-high-tech environment. The physical layout was as simple as it was functional. Seated on a raised platform centered along one of the long sides were the three ICC judges, with the presiding judge in the middle. Seated to the left of the judges was the prosecution team. To the right of the judges was the defense team, and behind them sat the accused. Located directly across the room from the judges were the witness bench and witness stand. Above the witness bench, the public gallery, accommodating two hundred and twenty people, was situated behind a large glass wall that allowed for the public to see in the courtroom, but not for those in the courtroom to see out.

As morning broke on this new day, the prosecution team, UN guards, and all manner of Court personnel were in attendance for the pretrial hearing. George Bush, wearing the same clothes in which he had played golf in St. Andrews, sat in the accused's chair. The public gallery was packed. Per protocol, the Court's clerk stood and announced in both English and French, "The International Criminal Court is now in session. All rise." All in the courtroom did except George Bush.

The presiding judge assigned to the case, the honorable and highly esteemed Harrison Hurst-Brown from Great Britain, walked briskly toward his seat at the judge's table wearing an ankle-length navy blue robe accentuated by purple stripes that ran from shoulder to foot and around both forearms. All ICC judges wear such robes. All other Court participants wear similar robes, except in black. Only the accused and the witnesses are allowed in Court not wearing robes. They wear street clothes.

Judge Hurst-Brown sat, as did all others. He looked around the courtroom to ensure that all was in order and then began with a noticeable hint of ceremony. "Good day, everybody. Mr. Bush, welcome to the International Criminal Court."

Bush, refusing to acknowledge the judge, said nothing and looked away.

Hurst-Brown continued, "When the ICC was created, it provided for three categories of international crimes to be investigated and prosecuted as and when necessary: genocide, crimes against humanity, and war crimes. George Bush, you are here to stand trial for war crimes in connection with the Iraq War, March 2003 through December 2011.

"The ICC has very strict protocol regarding the administration of justice. The question of jurisdiction is an initial and fundamental question of every case in international law. It is true, unfortunately, that the United States is not a member of the ICC. Neither is Iraq, for that matter. However, the Rome Statute provides that a nonmember state, such as Iraq, may accept jurisdiction—and I specifically refer to Article 12(3) of the Rome Statue—by a 'declaration lodged with the Registrar, accept the exercise of jurisdiction by the Court.' The sovereign state of Iraq has lodged such a declaration, and the ICC has accepted jurisdiction in connection with crimes that may or may not have been committed during the Iraq War. It is important to add, however, that the ICC accepts such jurisdiction on an ad hoc basis. For the avoidance of doubt, 'ad hoc' means 'without consideration to wider application'—in other words, a case that does not relate to, or create, precedent.

"According to the prosecution's investigation and the Pre-Trial Chamber's findings, the ICC is satisfied that the crimes with which you, George W. Bush, are charged have been correctly brought within the jurisdiction of the Court. It is a fundamental pillar of international criminal law that every person is entitled to select his or her legal counsel, commonly referred to as the 'defense' or 'defense team.' At this point in the proceedings, Mr. Bush, you have a choice to make, and the ICC will abide by whatever you choose. You can elect to be represented by your chosen legal counsel, in which case we will suspend any further activity until such time as they have arrived here in The Hague and you have had ample opportunity to consult with them privately to determine the course of your defense. A second option is that you can elect to defend yourself, commonly referred to as 'self-representation.' Would you like to make that determination now, or would you like to have some time to consider the matter?"

Bush sat stoically silent, only staring at Judge Hurst-Brown.

"Mr. Bush, which will it be: select a defense team, or self-represent, or be accorded time to consider the question?"

The former president and the ICC judge stared at each other for a long moment before Bush answered, "I've considered the question and here's my answer: this is bullshit. I know all about the ICC, its pluses and minuses. Don't forget I was the president of the United States of America for eight years and performed my solemn duty to protect and defend my country in a way that was entirely appropriate under the circumstances at the time. I also know that the former ICC prosecutor—what's his name, starts with 'O'?"

"Luis Moreno-Ocampo."

"Yes, Mr. Ocampo has already conducted a thorough review of all charges alleged against me and ruled that no activity committed during the Iraq War could be prosecuted by the ICC. I trust you are aware of these findings?"

Hurst-Brown adopted a more combative tone. "I am indeed aware of these findings but respectfully disagree with your conclusion. Mr. Ocampo did not 'rule' that there couldn't be prosecution, but rather that the case couldn't be prosecuted at that time because neither the United States nor Iraq was a member state of the ICC. I would remind you, sir, that Mr. Ocampo's opinion was rendered in 2006, only three years into a war that lasted eight years. During the nearly five years between the time Ocampo released his conclusions and the end of the war, hundreds of thousands more Iraqis and coalition forces died. Simply put, with more deaths resulting from that war, more time was needed to consider its legality. Furthermore, Article 15 of the Rome Statute provides that prior conclusions made by the Court may be reviewed in light of new facts or evidence. The Iraq War ended December 2011. Over time, additional information has been found which may well influence the prosecution's opinion of that war as it relates to war crimes and possibly other crimes."

Hurst-Brown paused for a moment to see if Bush would comment. He didn't. The judge pressed on. "Mr. Bush, how do you answer the question: select a defense team of your own choosing or self-represent?"

All attention was riveted on Bush. "My answer is that I am a citizen of the United States of America. And citizens of the United States are not subject to ICC investigation or prosecution. My actions were well known by the American people, Congress, the Supreme Court, and the United Nations, all of which concurred that my decisions during the Iraq War, including the removal of one of the most evil dictators the world has ever known, were not only justifiable but necessary. My answer is that I will not stand for this absurd, unjustified, maybe even illegal activity being proposed by the ICC. My activities as president of the United States relative to the Iraq War were performed in accordance with United States law—the law of the land. I'm not some outlaw gunslinger you can bring in here for a lynch mob hanging. Be careful how you respond, Mr. Judge, because you yourself will be held accountable for your actions as well."

Hurst-Brown countered with growing impatience, "My name, Mr. Bush, is Hurst-Brown. The International Criminal Court is comprised of member states representing the majority of the peoples of the world. It has a specifically prescribed due process of law that we will follow whether you approve or not. Now, as you have declined your right to assemble a defense team, it leaves you to defend yourself, and we will proceed accordingly. The Court will now inform you of your rights as an accused."

Left with no apparent option, Bush stood. "But, sir, I am not knowledgeable about international criminal law."

"Then you should engage defense counsel."

Neither the judge nor the accused spoke until Bush broke the stalemate. "Under great protest and with the admission of nothing, you leave me no choice but to assemble a defense team."

That said, Hurst-Brown rapped his gavel and announced, "The Court will recess until Mr. Bush's defense team has arrived at the ICC and has had appropriate time to confer with their client." Rapping his gavel a final time, he concluded the day's session. "*The Prosecutor v. George W. Bush* is adjourned until further notice."

Some days such as this yield so much story content that news organizations have to scramble to gather and report it all coherently.

France 24 was first to report. "It was a historic day in international criminal law as for the first time a former leader of a superpower was brought to the International Criminal Court to face criminal charges," political commentator Paulette Coblence began. "This was a day that many legal pundits thought would never come. Some historical perspective might be useful to understand the gravitas of the occasion. Following the horrible world wars of the twentieth century, peace-loving peoples around the world began to advocate forcefully for the creation of international criminal law, which would ultimately stand above and have force over national law. Specific elements such as jurisdiction, selection of crimes to be tried, judicial process to determine guilt or innocence, all needed to be debated and agreed upon.

"After much deliberation, the consensus opinion of participating countries was drafted into something called the Rome Statute. The United Nations' request to adapt the statute was submitted to all countries of the world. One hundred and thirty-nine participated in the decision, and the statute was voted into force July 2002. The stage was set for the creation of the first International Criminal Court.

"During the negotiations the United States made a few helpful contributions, but in the end it was apparently unhappy with the scope of power accorded to the ICC and did not join. Many around the world understood that to mean the United States simply did not want its citizens to be subjected to international legal jurisdiction.

"Over time, many Americans softened in their opposition to the ICC such that in the final hours of his last day as president, Bill Clinton signed the Rome Statute, making the United States a member state. Immediately upon taking office, George W. Bush approached the UN to see if the Clinton signature could be revoked. While international law does not permit a treaty to be 'unsigned,' the Vienna Convention does allow for a state to change its mind after signature. Mr. Bush's legal eagles quickly withdrew America's signature via a diplomatic note to the UN, declaring, 'in connection with the Rome Statute of the International Criminal Court . . . the United States does not intend to become a party to the treaty.'

"Regrettably for some, if not many, this stance taken by Mr. Bush as president of the United States has not changed."

Five minutes later in the time zone west of France, the BBC offered an interview hosted by Elizabeth Reynolds. "The ICC has tried many cases over the years with some notable success, such as the sentencing of Radovan Karadzic to forty years in prison for his role in ethnic cleansing in the former Yugoslavia and the slaughter of eight thousand Muslims in Srebrenica. But none are more important than this case against former president Bush. How could it be that a former leader of the free world could find himself standing trial at the ICC for war crimes? Joining me now to answer that question is Sir Nigel Pemberton, a renowned British solicitor and friend to the friendless in London's criminal justice system.

"Sir Nigel, while your experience these days is primarily in the Old Bailey, you have in the past defended some nasty characters in international criminal tribunals. How did the ICC get its hands on a former president of the United States?"

"Well, Elizabeth," Sir Nigel began, "even 'nasty characters,' as you call them, are entitled to a spirited defense, and I am sure former president Bush will get one here. While the United States is not a member of the ICC, international law stipulates that if a sovereign country accepts the jurisdiction of the ICC, even though it is not a member of the ICC, the ICC may in fact proceed with the case. In this instance, Iraq, which is not a member state, has accepted ICC jurisdiction in connection with Mr. Bush's alleged war crimes during the Iraq War. There are actually two other ways in which ICC jurisdiction could have been triggered in this case: first, if the UN Security Council had referred the case to the ICC, or second and perhaps less likely, if the United States had become a member state of the ICC. Neither of these occurred. And so, as there is no statute of limitations on the prosecution of war crimes, the case against Mr. Bush has begun."

Ms. Reynolds pressed him for more. "So what is the overarching significance of this move by the ICC to try a former president of the United States?"

"My goodness, Elizabeth, the significance cannot be overstated. Up until now, only heads or former heads of minor states have been subjected to international criminal law—Charles Taylor from Liberia, Slobodan Milošević from Serbia, Omar al-Bashir from Sudan, and others. Those are relatively minor characters in small countries. The United States is the most super of superpowers. The legitimacy of the International Criminal Court will indeed be on trial here, alongside Mr. Bush."

Even with the monumentally important responsibility the ICC has to uphold the rule of law on an international scale, it does not have a dedicated military force to defend itself. It must rely on UN security forces and a variety of local forces in The Hague. And so it was that the ICC had to deal, for the first time in its existence, with an attack by an angry nation—an angry superpower, no less.

After gathering at the USAG Wiesbaden Army base near Frankfurt, Germany, a team of twenty finely trained and well-equipped US Special Operations Forces (SOF) under the command of Marine captain Richard Rattigan boarded four Bell UH-1Y Venom helicopters and headed for the ICC with the urgent intent of rescuing former president Bush.

Following landings on the wide, rocky beaches of Scheveningen under the cover of night, the SOF team quietly deplaned, spread out, and traversed the one-kilometer journey to the ICC Detention Centre.

Immediately upon their arrival at the detention center, a firefight broke out. The Americans had encountered the well-trained, well-armed, permanent UN security force whose job it is to protect the ICC. Loud, rapid, concussive rounds fired by both sides shattered the peace and quiet of the night. Whatever hopes the Americans had of a successful stealth rescue were ruptured in seconds.

Inside the detention center, security forces manned their battle stations to repel the invading forces. George Bush heard the gunfire and knew exactly what was happening. Four UN guards entered his cell, handcuffed and gagged him, lowered him to the floor, and lay on top of him. If anyone was to rescue George Bush, they would have to do so over the guards' dead bodies, literally.

Outside, US SOF were engaged in soldier-to-soldier combat with ICC security forces. Captain Rattigan was exchanging close-range fire with a UN soldier. After a few volleys, Rattigan came to a startling realization. He knew the soldier across from him. He was Edmond Heathcott, from England. They had fought side by side in Iraq. A variety of thoughts flooded Rattigan's mind: (1) The intel he had been given didn't sufficiently describe how formidable a garrison the new ICC Detention Centre was. (2) A successful rescue attempt would require a much bigger force, armed with more weaponry. (3) Pursuing this attack any harder might create a monumental diplomatic problem for the United States, if it hadn't already. (4) Even if they could rescue Bush, he might get hit or even killed in the cross fire of his own escape. (5) How could he and Heathcott fight each other, having fought so valiantly *side by side* in Iraq?

After four minutes of nonstop shooting, the Americans ceased fire. Defying strict military protocol, Rattigan called out to his friend, "Edmond, is that you?"

Following an awkward moment of silence, Heathcott responded, "Yes. Tell me it's not you, Richard."

"'Fraid so."

"This is one hell of an awkward development."

"Yes."

Heathcott paused before his next question. "What are you doing, as if I had to ask?"

"You know."

"You can't have him."

"Wrong thing to say, Ed. You know that."

"Think about it, Richard—a handful of American soldiers fighting a small army of UN troops? You're not going to get him and the attempt is not worth the lives of your soldiers."

As much as Rattigan hated it, he realized what Heathcott said was the simple truth and gave the order for his men to retreat, which they did.

Inside the detention center, George Bush lay back in his bed, resigned to the fact that he would, after all, have to face trial for his role in the Iraq War.

CHAPTER FIVE

The Cavalry Arrives

Words have the power to both destroy and heal. When
words are both true and kind, they can change our world.
—Gautama Buddha

The three members of George Bush's defense team waited in a room in the detention center specifically designed for private prisoner-attorney meetings. The room was windowless and empty except for a rectangular table, eight chairs, and two wastebaskets. No guards. No phones. No recording devices. Double-thick walls prevented noise seepage. Seated and reviewing legal briefs were defense attorneys Meredith Lott and Jonathan Ortloff. The lead defense attorney, Edward Jamison White III, was up and pacing.

Ed White and George Bush met and became good buddies in Houston, Texas, when Bush was working in a mentoring program in the poverty-stricken Third Ward, and White, who had just graduated from the University of Texas with honors, was cultivating his dreams of becoming a big-time Texas lawyer. Later, when Bush was governor, he assigned White to the prestigious Texas Land Office, where the lawyer worked tirelessly to help fund Texas public schools and provide needed benefits to Texas veterans. Their early fondness morphed into a lifelong friendship that included wives, kids, deer hunting, baseball, and the odd business venture.

The door opened. A UN detention guard nodded at former president Bush, who nodded in return and entered. White regarded his old friend carefully as he walked over to first shake his hand and then give him a big hug.

"Greetings," Bush said with some relief. "Sorry to have to drag you over here."

"More to the point, we're sorry they dragged *you* over here. It's the most preposterous thing I've ever heard."

Bush smiled warmly. "I know how you love your Texas Longhorns during football season. Think they can manage without you?"

White chuckled. "They'll manage, probably better. We have bigger fish to fry." He gestured to his colleagues. "George, I'd like to introduce you to the other two members of your team. Both are extraordinary defense attorneys with impressive credentials—and more importantly, schooled and experienced in international criminal law."

Bush greeted the other attorneys. "Thanks for coming."

"Meredith Lott is the top international criminal law attorney at Hurst, Rosenfeld, and Felps in Washington, DC. Graduated Phi Beta Kappa from the University of Southern California and first in her class at Stanford Law. She's a specialist in international extradition and a black belt in karate. Most folks don't mess with her too much."

Bush offered his hand to shake. "Black belt in karate, my kind of girl."

White continued his no-nonsense introductions. "Jonathan Ortloff. Graduated Notre Dame, summa cum laude. His PhD on

'The Creation and Functionality of the International Criminal Court' was published in top law reviews in the United States, Great Britain, and elsewhere in the free world. Jonathan started a boutique law firm in Manhattan that specializes in international law and is a plus-two handicap at Winged Foot. So when we extricate you from this quagmire, you can have him as a partner and then maybe I will have to pay you, instead of the other way around, which is usually the case."

Bush shook Ortloff's hand heartily. "Killer attorney and plus-two handicap. Where have you been all my life?"

"George, rest assured you've got a million watts of intellectual capacity here to defend you," White stated confidently.

"I don't think this is going to be a fair fight."

"I'm sure the prosecution thinks otherwise. Mind if we jump right in?"

"Can't tell you how much I've been looking forward to doing just that."

They settled into chairs. Ed White looked compassionately at his friend. "First of all, how you doing?"

"I've been better. How the hell can we get me out of here and how quickly can we do it?"

"'Not sure' to the first question, and 'soon as legally possible' to the second. We need to discuss a number of items, including ICC protocol and which witnesses to call in your defense, but first I want Meredith and Jonathan to share their thoughts as they relate to the case in general."

"Okay, bombs away."

"Meredith, you first."

Meredith smiled. "Mr. President . . . may I call you Mr. Bush or George?"

"George will do."

"First, I'd like to say that my family have loved and supported your family since I was a little girl, and my support for you personally has never wavered."

"Thank you."

"Knowing what you knew at the time, I would've waged war on Iraq as well."

"Gratifying to hear, especially considering the circumstances."

"Next, I'd like to state that, in my opinion, the actions taken by the International Criminal Court in general, and the prosecutors specifically, are in blatant breach of international legal agreements and violate well-established ethical protocol. Simply put, it is offensive, obnoxious, rude, and arrogant."

Bush had listened carefully and responded with one word. "Good."

Next, Jonathan spoke. "Mr. Bush—George—for openers I'd like to state that the charges alleged against you are not consistent with the generally held understanding of what constitutes war crimes. Furthermore, we have investigated the prosecuting attorneys, McBride and Shadid, and regard them to be inadequate in terms of having the requisite experience or gravitas to effectively prosecute this case, which encompasses massive legal doctrine and bears the potential of groundbreaking and precedent-setting legal implications."

Bush raised his eyebrows. "Meaning?"

"Meaning they don't have a chance in hell of making their accusations stick. Meaning we are going to kick their asses."

Bush smiled at his lead attorney and stated emphatically, "Shit, Ed, these guys can play on my team any day."

White responded, "Understood. I wouldn't want to try a case against these two assassins if I could possibly avoid it." Then

White transitioned to another important concern. "George, I'm sure you're wondering how Laura is doing."

"More than wondering."

"She's doing okay. We've been in almost hourly contact with her. She's pissed off as hell, but more worried about how you're doing."

"When's she getting here?"

"Soon as possible. Twenty-four hours, plus or minus."

"I'm missing her."

"No doubt," White said with as much compassion as he could muster, and continued. "Now I'd like to lay out our step-by-step offensive strategy to build your defense. First we'll start by . . ."

CHAPTER SIX

Facing the Music

Peace does not mean an absence of conflicts;
differences will always be there. Peace means solving
these differences through peaceful means;
through dialogue, education, knowledge;
and through humane ways.

—Dalai Lama XIV

After a week of schooling George Bush in international law—advising him on ICC courtroom procedure and decorum, stressing the need to state only the information asked of him and not volunteer anything more—the defense team notified the judges that they were ready to proceed.

Three days later, on a crisp October morning, the case was scheduled to resume. But early that morning all participants were notified that one of the judges assigned to the Bush case, Judge Miyako Kimura from Japan, had learned that her granddaughter in Tokyo had committed suicide. Unofficial word spread that the young woman was an honors student in law school who had been battling with drugs and could no longer deal with the conflicting pressures of her life. As many involved in the case had sons and daughters, and some had grandsons and granddaughters, the news was horrific—the proverbial bitter pill to swallow.

Out of respect for Judge Kimura, the case was rescheduled to start midday the following day. And so it did.

There was a decidedly different mood when George Bush entered the courtroom this day. He was no longer alone in his defense but was now girded by a threesome of impressive, high-octane, highly intelligent defense attorneys.

Presiding judge Harrison Hurst-Brown began the day in a quiet, reflective tone. "As we reconvene this trial, the Court wishes to extend our deepest sympathies to Judge Kimura, express to her that we feel her pain, and thank her for her courage in being willing to attend Court to ensure the administration of international law continues uninterrupted." He paused for a moment to allow his comments to register in the room and then continued, "Mr. Bush, we want to be sure you have had ample time to discuss the case with your defense team and are ready to proceed."

"Yes, sir," Bush answered. "Ready to go."

Ed White took over. "Your Honor and fellow judges, my name is Edward White. I'm Mr. Bush's lead defense attorney."

Hurst-Brown nodded. "Mr. White, the Court welcomes you and your colleagues and asks if you have had sufficient time to meet and discuss the case with your client."

"Yes, Your Honors. And with due respect, we wish to state that the ICC has already committed serious breaches of international law. Your abduction of a former president of the United States and transference against his will to the ICC is in direct violation of both international and national laws. Next, I specifically refer you to Article 22(2) of the Rome Statute that relates to the principle of jurisdiction. It states, 'In case of *ambiguity*, the definition shall be interpreted *in favor of the person being investigated*, prosecuted or convicted.' Not only is this case *ambiguous*; it is a clear misapplication of justice. We hereby request the immediate release of Mr. Bush, after which we will be filing criminal charges against those who are responsible for these outlandish and illegal acts, including the chief prosecutor, you yourselves the judges of the ICC, and others as warranted."

"Thank you, Mr. White," Hurst-Brown responded, as if he'd heard it all before. "We have already addressed the question of jurisdiction in great detail. Unless you have anything new to add, this Court will proceed with what it was created to do."

White amped up the rhetoric. "We are very disappointed to hear and note how entrenched you already seem to be, Your Honor. But so be it. We now move to the merits of this case. Mr. Bush's sovereign immunity as a former president of the United States stands as a preemptive block against this prosecution. Sovereign immunity has been regarded as a nonnegotiable element of international law since Roman times. Moreover, there is the well-established legal concept known as the War Powers Resolution, which provides that the president of the United States, in his role of commander in chief, has the power to repel attacks against his country and his people. It also contemplates and embraces a reasonable loss of human life attendant to the use of armed forces in pursuit of military objectives. You cannot bring a former president of the United States before this tribunal and try him for official acts he performed while in office."

Hurst-Brown seemed only too willing to engage in this debate. "Mr. White, the overriding concept in force here is that Mr. Bush is a *former* head of state, not a *sitting* head of state. Furthermore, you must know that crimes included under the ICC's definition of war crimes have *no statute of limitations*. Now, as there is much to do, Mr. White, I suggest we get on with the business of this Court."

White stood resolute next to his client. "Your Honors, we wish to provide warning to this Court that the eyes of the world are on this case, and state emphatically that we consider the Court's actions against Mr. Bush to be in violation of well-established international law and a breach of his fundamental human rights. We intend to deal with each of these matters in the fullness of time."

"Your warning is duly noted, Mr. White," Hurst-Brown commented and moved on. "It is important for all involved to note that henceforth the defendant in this case, Mr. George W. Bush, will be referred to as 'the accused,' and that the term is neutral with regard to guilt or innocence."

"Your Honor, excuse me," White interrupted again. "The man you now refer to as 'the accused' is in fact a kind and decent man. He and his mother, father, and brother are highly regarded patriotic citizens of the United States. Mr. Bush served honorably as the forty-third president of United States. He is not a criminal. He is not a murderer. He is not a ruthless dictator.

"The president of the United States is charged with making many challenging and often controversial decisions. He must make those decisions based on what he believes to be in the best interest of the people. Here at the ICC you have dealt with Mr. Bush as if he were a deranged mass murderer— a Slobodan Milošević, a Joseph Kony, or even an Adolf Hitler. This treatment has resulted in an intensely unfounded and unfair characterization of Mr. Bush which is highly offensive to all Americans."

If Hurst-Brown was irritated by White's declarations, he didn't show it. "Mr. White, thank you for your personal opinions. But the law is not concerned with whatever else a man may or may not have done in his life. Justice is blind. Those of us who are charged with upholding the law seek only the accurate application of the law. Now, with respect, this Court will proceed with the discharge of its solemn duties. Have a seat, Mr. White."

White considered his options and sat.

Hurst-Brown continued. "The first fundamental element of international law is that the accused must be present at trial, which he is. All cases start with a presumption of innocence. The Rome Statute imposes the burden of proof upon the prosecution, meaning it must prove guilt beyond reasonable doubt. The accused is entitled to a fair, impartial, public, and speedy trial. He or she has the right to assemble a defense team of his or her choosing, which has occurred. Furthermore, the accused has the right not to testify against himself or to confess guilt. The silence of the accused cannot be considered in the determination of guilt or innocence. The accused and/or his counsel will be provided ample time to rebut and refute all claims. He and/or his counsel can cross-examine witnesses and contest evidence.

"If the accused is found guilty of one or more of the crimes identified within the scope of war crimes, the Court has available the following forms of punishment: first, an admonishment; second, imprisonment of up to thirty years, to which may be added a fine; and third, an admonishment, imprisonment, and possible fine. In extreme cases justified by the gravity of the crime or crimes, the Court may impose a term of life imprisonment. However, under no circumstance is this Court able to render the death penalty.

"The decision of this Court will be rendered by a majority vote of its three presiding judges, whom I'd like to introduce for the record at this time: Judge Miyako Kimura from Japan, Judge Omolade Bankole from Nigeria, and I am Harrison Hurst-Brown of the United Kingdom.

"Now, Mr. Bush, the Court would like to provide you with the opportunity to make any comments or ask any questions."

Bush and White exchanged looks, after which White responded. "Other than what's already been stated, Mr. Bush has nothing to say at this time. His defense will have many questions in due course."

"Duly noted, Mr. White. Consistent with ICC protocol, the clerk is handing Mr. Bush and defense counsel a document containing the charges that fully define the crimes of which Mr. Bush is accused. Article 8 of the ICC Statute sets forth the definition of war crimes as 'any of the following acts against persons or property protected under the provisions of the relevant Geneva Convention' including: willful killing; torture or inhuman treatment; willfully causing great suffering, or serious injury to body or health; intentionally launching an attack in the knowledge that such attack will cause incidental loss of life or injury to civilians or damage to civilian objects or widespread, long-term and severe damage to the natural environment; attacking or bombarding towns, villages, dwellings or buildings which are undefended and which are not military objectives; willfully depriving prisoners of war the rights of fair and regular trial; and intentionally directing attacks against the civilian population not taking direct part in hostilities.

"Now, per Article 64(8)(a), we afford Mr. Bush the opportunity to make an admission of guilt."

"Your Honor, Mr. Bush will make no such admission."

"Very well, so be it. Before the prosecution team begins, I'd like to inform Mr. Bush and defense counsel that he or it may object to the charges, and/or challenge the evidence presented by the prosecution, and/or present evidence of its own."

"With respect, Your Honor, we also wish to submit a formal objection to the prosecuting attorneys."

"On what grounds?"

"Bias. Mr. McBride is an American and Ms. Shadid is an Iraqi. They cannot help but be biased in this case by their nationalities. We request reassignment of this case to more neutral staffing within the Office of the Prosecutor."

Hurst-Brown seemed to be running out of patience. "Need I remind you, Mr. White, that the Office of the Prosecutor is an independent organ within the ICC and, as such, the chief prosecutor may decide which of his deputies will try any given case? Disqualifications based solely upon nationality are not permitted."

The back-and-forth contentious clatter between the lead defense attorney and the presiding judge ratcheted up the energy in the courtroom. These were opposing forces at the tops of their games advocating aggressively for their positions. Hurst-Brown advanced the proceedings to the next phase. "The Court now recognizes the prosecution in the case of *The Prosecutor v. George W. Bush.*"

Prosecution attorney Nadia Shadid stood ready and resolute before the Court. Her demeanor inside the courtroom was much different from that on the outside. In her personal life she appeared rather fragile and gentle, but in court she evidenced strength, intelligence, and supreme confidence. With a nod to the judges she began, "Your Honors, Mr. Bush, members of the defense, ICC clerk and staff, greetings, all. My name is Nadia Shadid. I am from Fallujah in the Iraqi province of Al Anbar, sixty miles outside Baghdad. All of us who care about the International Criminal Court, past, present, and future, are very pleased to have this magnificent new building in which to conduct our business. As one might expect, the ICC courtrooms are equipped with state-of-the-art digital equipment. As there have been an unprecedented number of requests from press outlets around the world for coverage of this trial, for the first time the ICC is providing 'live' real-time audio and video coverage of the proceedings. Following the trial, a complete audio-video recording and written transcript of the proceedings will be made available to any and all upon request."

Turning to address the judges, she continued. "Your Honors, now that we have informed all parties of this coverage, as required by law, we request the Court's permission to commence production of the feed."

"The Court is supportive of providing such live coverage so that interested parties around the world can monitor the case as it happens in real time," Hurst-Brown stated proudly. "The Court approves commencement of the international feed. Thank you, Ms. Shadid."

There was a brief pause as Shadid glanced up above the public gallery to the newly created ICC media room, where technicians flipped the switch to engage this new technology and then flashed a thumbs-up to Shadid as her cue to continue. "Thank you, Your Honor. Opening statement from the prosecution will continue from my colleague, Mr. Michael McBride."

Shadid offered an encouraging smile to McBride as she sat and he stood to address the bench. "Thank you, Your Honors." Then, turning to the courtroom, "Mr. Bush, members of the defense team, clerks, guards, courtroom attendants . . . greetings. To begin, and to state the obvious, we all must disabuse ourselves of any preconceived idea that just because a man is the president of the United States he is incapable of committing a crime or is immune to international law. That, of course, would have no foundation in logic or law. What follows is the chronological event-by-event story of what George W. Bush did and said in his capacity as president of the United States and commander in chief to 'cause' the Iraq War to happen, bearing in mind that all human lives lost, damage to physical structures, prisoner maltreatment, and torture are the direct result of this war. Obviously, had Mr. Bush not caused the war to happen, all the men and women killed in the war might still be alive, those injured physically and/or mentally would presumably still be well, and the damaged or destroyed physical structures would still be standing. Incidental loss of civilian life and damage to civilian property would not have occurred. And, as there would have been no prisoners, there would have been no prisoner abuse.

"Now, for the orientation of those interested in the facts of this case, I'd like to identify two entirely separate entities: first is the group known as al Qaeda, led by Osama bin Laden, and second, the government of Iraq, led by its elected president, Saddam Hussein. Al Qaeda was and is a militant Islamic organization founded by bin Laden. Its origins trace back to Arab volunteers who fought against the Soviet invasion of Afghanistan in the 1980s. Not only did bin Laden found al Qaeda; he remained its leader until his death in 2011.

"Entirely separate and apart from al Qaeda is the Iraqi government and its president Saddam Hussein. In Iraq's election before the Iraq War, Saddam Hussein received the preponderance of votes from his people, despite the Western world's disdain for their election process. Like many in the Western world, I think Saddam Hussein was one of the most disgusting and reprehensible people who ever walked on Earth. But he served Iraq as its president for twenty-four years. If he was a devil, he was Iraq's devil. As will be clearly proven, al Qaeda and bin Laden had no working relationship with Iraq and Saddam Hussein. They were headquartered in different countries. They were never

coconspirators or coperpetrators in any activity. In fact, if anything, they were each the enemy of the other.

"Now, the prosecution will tell the story that lays out the
foundation of this case. This is the story of how George Bush is
personally responsible for creating the pretext for, and then waging, the Iraq War—and the devastating results of his war. As
much was said and done by Mr. Bush—and caused to happen by
Mr. Bush—we will focus on those incidents that most specifically implicate him in these crimes.

"As a prelude to this narrative, I'd like to mention a man by
the name of Richard Clarke. At the beginning of the twenty-
first century, Mr. Clarke was considered to be America's foremost authority on terror and as such knew more about Osama
bin Laden and al Qaeda—and Saddam Hussein and Iraq—than
anyone in America. Only days after Bush's inauguration in January
2001, Clarke requested an urgent meeting with the president to discuss plans to go after the greatest threat to America at the time,
al Qaeda and its leader, Osama bin Laden. Mr. Bush, either too
busy or not interested, never granted the meeting. Let's stop
and think about that for a moment: A newly elected president
of the United States refused to meet his top counterterrorism
expert regarding the most urgent threat against America. Why?
Why wasn't George Bush interested in hearing about this most
immediate threat to the country he was just elected to protect?
Answers to such questions will emerge during the course of this
trial."

McBride, gaining momentum, continued with more zeal.
"Your Honors, the prosecution wishes to call the attention of the
Court to Prosecution Evidence #1, which is a chronicle record of
the activities of Mr. Bush from September 11, 2001, to March
20, 2003 . . . the day of the 9/11 attacks to the day of the US

invasion of Iraq. As we refer to each of these activities, pertinent information will be displayed on the monitors located around the courtroom and can be found in the binders of evidence that have been provided. And so we begin.

"September 11, 2001, the very night of the 9/11 attacks. The World Trade Center was reduced to rubble and the Pentagon was still burning. George Bush finally did meet with Richard Clarke in the Situation Room of the White House. Mr. Bush said to Mr. Clarke, 'I know you have a lot to do and all, but I want you, as soon as you can, to go back over everything. *See if Saddam did this.* See if he's linked in any way.' Clarke responded, 'But, Mr. President, al Qaeda did this,' to which Mr. Bush replied, 'I know. But see if Saddam was involved. Just look. I want to know.' 'Absolutely, we will look,' Clarke said, and continued, 'But you know we have looked several times for state sponsorship of al Qaeda and not found any real linkages to Iraq.' Then, according to Clarke, Mr. Bush said testily, 'Look into Iraq, Saddam,' and walked away.

"After complying with Mr. Bush's requests to look into the matter, Mr. Clarke submitted a report signed by him and cosigned by all relevant intelligence agencies, including the Federal Bureau of Investigation and the Central Intelligence Agency, stating that there was *no evidence of Iraqi involvement in 9/11.*

"September 21, 2001, ten days after 9/11. Mr. Bush received a classified President's Daily Brief, known as a PDB, indicating that his intelligence team had found *no solid evidence linking Saddam Hussein to the September 11 attacks* and that, and I'm quoting from the PDB, 'There was scant credible evidence that Iraq had any significant collaborative ties with al Qaeda.' I repeat for clarification and emphasis, ten days after the attacks on September 11, the defendant received a written report signed by top intelligence officers that stated there was no solid evidence Saddam Hussein or Iraq had any involvement in 9/11, and that there was no creditable evidence that Iraq had any ties with al Qaeda.

"November 21, 2001, two months and ten days after the 9/11 attacks. During a National Security Council meeting in the White House, Mr. Bush asked Secretary of Defense Donald Rumsfeld to review existing battle plans for Iraq. Quoting Bush: 'What kind of war plan do you have for Iraq?' Rumsfeld said he would look into it. Then Mr. Bush said, 'And get Tommy Franks looking at what it would take to protect America by removing Saddam Hussein if we have to.' Please note it was on this day, November 21, 2001—two months and ten days after the 9/11 attacks, and one year, four months before the invasion of Iraq—that George Bush first put into motion the series of events that would lead to his war.

"December 28, 2001, three months and seventeen days after 9/11. At the Bush Prairie Chapel Ranch in Crawford, Texas, Mr. Bush met with CIA director George Tenet, Secretary of Defense Rumsfeld, and US Army general Tommy Franks. Bush asked about war plans with Iraq. General Franks answered, 'Mr. President, our current plan for Iraq is called Operations Plan 1003. We have a lot to do on this thing, but let me show you where we are with this right now.' The plan was the beginning of a new war strategy for Iraq. After hearing Franks's plan, Mr. Bush turned to CIA director Tenet and said, 'Your people have done a good job in Afghanistan. What do you have in Iraq?' Mr. Tenet answered, 'Iraq's a different situation, sir. Our intelligence capacity is thin and we've got a credibility problem.' Mr. Bush pressed him, 'There have been no UN inspectors in Iraq since 1998. We don't know what kind of weapons they've developed, and we don't know Saddam's intentions. But we do know he used WMD before on the Iranians and on his own people. We cannot allow weapons of mass destruction to fall into the hands of terrorists.'"

McBride turned to the ICC judges and, apparently wanting to ensure they were fully engaged, looked at each of them, eye to eye, while saying, "Your Honors, please note that three and a half months after 9/11, George Bush was all but ignoring bin Laden, and instead was shifting the focus to Saddam Hussein, even though he was informed Saddam had nothing to do with 9/11. Moving on." He turned back to address the courtroom.

"February 6, 2002, one year, one month, and fourteen days before the war. A 2000 National Intelligence Estimate, or NIE, given to Mr. Bush reported the following: 'We have *low confidence* in our ability to assess when Saddam would use WMD,' and 'we have *little specific information* on Iraq's chemical weapons stockpile.' On the issue of nuclear weapons, the NIE report stated, *'Iraq does not yet have a nuclear weapon or sufficient material to make one.'"*

McBride raised his voice and said to everyone listening inside the Court and around the world, "Please take note. One year and one month before initiating the Iraq War, George Bush was told specifically and repeatedly that Saddam *was not a threat to the United States*, and none of the evidence established definitively that Saddam even had the capacity to harm the United States.

"February 7, 2002, one year, one month, and thirteen days before the war. Mr. Bush and his national security team met in the White House. General Franks summarized plans for a military offensive in Afghanistan to attack and destroy al Qaeda. Referring to bin Laden, Mr. Bush asked, 'Is he in there, Tommy?' Franks replied, 'The intel people think there's a possibility. The truth is, Mr. President, I'm not sure.' Then Mr. Bush moved on to war plans for Iraq. General Franks presented his refined plans. It was the first time Mr. Bush saw an actual plan that he could order carried out.

"April 4, 2002, eleven months, sixteen days before the war. At the White House, Mr. Bush participated in an interview with Trevor McDonald, a reporter for ITV television in the UK. In it Mr. Bush said, 'I made up my mind that Saddam needs to go. The policy of my government is that he goes.' McDonald responded, 'People think that Saddam Hussein has no links with the al Qaeda network and I'm wondering why you have—' Mr. Bush interrupted, 'The worst thing that could happen would be to allow a nation like Iraq run by Saddam Hussein to develop weapons of mass destruction and then team up with terrorist organizations so they can blackmail the world.' McDonald asked, 'How are you going to achieve this?' Bush replied, 'Wait and see.' McDonald responded, 'Whether he allows the inspectors in or not, he is the next target?' Bush answered, 'You're one of these clever report-ers that keeps trying to put words in my mouth. You've had my answer on the subject.'"

Ed White interjected, "Objection, Your Honors. Attempting to prejudice the Court with parenthetical issues that have noth-ing to do with this case."

Hurst-Brown nodded in agreement. "Objection sustained."

Undeterred, McBride pressed on. "Continuing with events that have everything to do with this case. August 5, 2002, seven months and fifteen days before the war. The White House. General Franks briefed Mr. Bush and the National Security Council on his new 'hybrid concept' for war in Iraq. Bush replied, 'I like the concept. We *need to have humanitarian assis-tance* on the battlefield from day one.'" Turning to the judges,

McBride continued, "Your Honors, this is important because it is evidence that the accused knew back in August of 2002 that the US military and coalition forces he would be sending into Iraq would inflict considerable human and physical damage—knowledge that proves Mr. Bush's 'criminal intent,' which is a necessary component in determining the guilt or innocence of war crimes."

McBride had waited for a long time to depose Bush and wasn't holding back. "That same night, August 5, 2002, Mr. Bush met with Secretary of State Colin Powell and National Security Advisor Condoleezza Rice in the White House. Secretary Powell, a decorated Army general with a public approval rating of 70 percent, was troubled. Quoting Secretary Powell: 'War could destabilize friendly regimes in Saudi Arabia, Egypt, and Jordan. War would take down Saddam and you will become the governing force until you get a new government. You break it, you own it. It's nice to say we can do it unilaterally, except you can't. If you think it's just a matter of picking up the phone and blowing a whistle and it goes . . . no, you need allies, you need access and whatnot. Worse, the United States, in perhaps the largest manhunt in history, has not found Osama bin Laden.' Mr. Bush listened for most of the two-hour meeting and then asked, 'What should I do?' Mr. Powell responded, 'You can still make a pitch for a coalition or UN action. If you take it to the UN, you've got to recognize that they might be able to solve it, in which case there is no war.'"

McBride again turned to address the judges directly. "Your Honors, not only did Mr. Bush refuse to listen to the advice of his respected secretary of state; he started an aggressive campaign to sell his war. Realizing the American people would never buy his head fake from bin Laden to Hussein, and from al Qaeda to Iraq, Mr. Bush turned to a smaller, more manageable audience—the United States Congress, the majority of whom were of his same political persuasion, Republican, and many of whom were his 'good buddies.'

"September 4, 2002, six months and sixteen days before the war. Mr. Bush met with eighteen key Senate and House members in the White House for the sole purpose of pitching his war. With the permission of the Court, I'd like to quote exactly what Mr. Bush said and then follow it with the truth: 'Iraq is on a lot of people's minds, because Saddam is *a serious threat to the United States* and his neighbors and his own citizens.' First, Saddam was not then, and had never been, a 'serious threat' to the United States. And if Saddam and Iraq were on the minds of the American people, it was because Mr. Bush kept mentioning both of them.

"Continuing to quote Mr. Bush: 'My administration embraces that policy *even more so in light of 9/11.*'"

McBride turned again to the judges to emphasize his point. "Please, Your Honors, there should be no doubts that George Bush *used the attacks of 9/11* to give credence to his war with Iraq, even though the one had absolutely nothing to do with the other. This was clear evidence of Mr. Bush's strategy. Here's an example of how it worked: Senator Don Nickles, Republican from Oklahoma, said to Bush, 'Mr. President . . . Congress adjourns October 11. Do you want us to vote before we leave?' Mr. Bush responded, 'Yes! I want you to have a debate. The issue isn't going away. You can't let it linger.' Translating 'political-speak' into real language, we can understand Mr. Bush's message: You can debate all you want, but I'm the president of the United States, and I say we're going to war with Iraq, and you better get off your asses and get it done because I'm getting impatient."

White interrupted. "Objection, Your Honors. Uncalled for and unflattering characterization of the defendant intended to prejudice the judges."

Hurst-Brown agreed. "Objection sustained. Mr. McBride, you will stick to the facts and withhold your personal interpretation of the events."

Sensing an opportunity to break the momentum and possibly the advantage the prosecution was gaining in the case, White offered the following: "Your Honors, given the lateness of the hour, defense requests a conclusion to the day's proceedings."

Hurst-Brown paused to consider the request, glanced over to his fellow judges, who nodded approvingly, and announced, "The Court agrees with the sentiments of the defense. Court adjourned until oh nine hundred tomorrow."

Later that night on an evening news program in Russia, one of its most respected political pundits, Anatoly Vetrov of NTV, offered the following: "The obvious explanation of why the United States is not a member of the ICC—even though its closest allies, including Great Britain, France, Australia, and Canada, are—must be that George Bush Jr. knew he would be committing crimes which would violate international law and didn't want to be subjected to the scrutiny of the ICC. The Bush case is significant because it could set a precedent that all leaders of all countries, whether members of the ICC or not, could in the future be held to the rigid standards of international criminal law."

This commentary was considered of particular interest because the list of nonsignatory states of the ICC—China, North Korea, Israel, Iran, Syria, and others—includes both the United States and Russia.

CHAPTER SEVEN

Resumption

*Violence is immoral because it thrives on hatred rather
than love. It destroys community and makes brotherhood
impossible. It leaves society in monologue rather than
dialogue. Violence ends up defeating itself. It creates
bitterness in the survivors and brutality in the destroyers.*
—Martin Luther King, Jr.

Following a night of heated discussion and debate internally among the teams of attorneys regarding the early going of the case, the Court reassembled at 09:00 the following day.

Intent on regaining his momentum from the previous day, prosecuting attorney Michael McBride began. "Your Honors, continuing with the litany of specific things done by the accused, George Bush, to cause the Iraq War, we call your attention to September 9, 2002, six months and eleven days before the invasion. A report was prepared for the Joint Chiefs of Staff entitled 'Iraq: Status of WMD Programs,' written by Air Force major general Glen Shaffer, head of the Joint Staff's intelligence team in 2002. Your Honors, prosecution would like to enter this report as Prosecution Evidence #2."

As McBride continued, Shadid handed the document to the clerk in order for it to be entered into the formal record.

"Keeping in mind this was written six and a half months before Mr. Bush sent America into war with Iraq, the report states the following: 'We don't know with any precision how much we don't know'; 'Our knowledge of the Iraqi weapons program *is based largely, perhaps 90 percent, on analysis of imprecise intelligence*'; 'Our assessments *rely heavily on analytic assumptions and judgment rather than hard evidence*'; 'We *do not know with confidence* the location of any nuclear-weapon-related facilities'; and finally 'We *cannot confirm* the identity of any Iraqi facilities that produce, test, fill, or store biological weapons.'

"Now, Mr. Bush," McBride said, turning to the former president, "I believe there's an old saying in Texas: 'If it looks like a skunk and smells like a skunk, then it's a skunk.' This report was commissioned by Secretary of Defense Donald Rumsfeld, and compiled by your Joint Chiefs' intelligence team. Information such as this makes it easy to understand why you may refuse to testify in this Court under oath, because when asked about it either you would have to admit you weren't aware of it—exposing gross dereliction of duty—or confess you were aware of it, which proves you waged the Iraq War for no good reason. I encourage you and your defense counsel to consider this. While you are within your rights not to testify, your silence may be perceived as an admission of guilt."

"Objection, Your Honors," White barked. "You have already instructed that under international law, refusal to testify is not to be considered an admission of guilt."

Hurst-Brown could only concur. "Objection sustained."

"Those who have nothing to hide and are convinced that the truth is on their side, are only too happy to testify in their defense," McBride noted and continued. "Moving on. September 19, 2002. Regardless of the intelligence information and obsessed with selling his war, Mr. Bush met with eleven other members of the House of Representatives. Again, here's what Mr. Bush said, followed by the truth. Bush: 'The biggest threat is Saddam Hussein and his weapons of mass destruction.' Fact: The last time there was any proof Saddam had WMD was in the mid-1990s. He certainly *did not have them in 2002* as Mr. Bush threatened he did—as was eventually, clearly, and abundantly proven by many reliable sources.

"Further quoting Mr. Bush: 'He'—referring to Saddam—'can blow up Israel and that would trigger an international conflict.' 'Blow up Israel'! Really? Under the circumstances that existed at that time, it would have been virtually impossible for Saddam to transport bomb tonnage sufficient to blow up Israel, even if he had it. Saddam had virtually no friends in the region to help with such an attack, having fought with most of them for years, and besides, many of them were friendly to the United States. Mr. Bush continued: 'We will take over the oil fields early and mitigate the oil shock.' This was another piece of Bush's strategy—use America's fear of an oil shortage in the Middle East and rising gas prices at home to convince the American people of the need for his war.

"September 26, 2002, five months and twenty-four days before the war. Mr. Bush met with eighteen more congressmen in the White House. He told them, 'Saddam Hussein is a terrible guy who is teaming up with al Qaeda.' Not so. We have already provided evidence that numerous government sources informed Mr. Bush in writing that neither Saddam nor Iraq had any connection to, or affiliation with, al Qaeda. What George Bush was telling US congressmen was not true. There was never any evidence connecting Saddam Hussein and Iraq to al Qaeda, which again means he had no legitimate reason to wage his war."

It was hard to tell whether defense attorney White's objections were *genuine* in the sense he felt McBride was out of bounds, or *cosmetic* in the sense he wanted to stop McBride's momentum. Nonetheless, he continued the practice. "Objection, Your Honors. It is totally preposterous that the prosecution could state such things so unequivocally without having firsthand access to secret classified government documents that would be available to a sitting president."

Hurst-Brown turned toward the prosecutor. "Mr. McBride, what say you?"

McBride responded instantly. "Following the Iraq War the United States government conducted two comprehensive investigations of what was known, when it was known, and by whom it was known. All information, classified or otherwise, is now publicly available. Furthermore, all principal players in and attendant to the White House at the time in question have published memoirs detailing what happened before, during, and after the war. These facts are known by anybody who bothers to look, regardless of the defense's attempt to make them appear to be obscure and/or classified. In light of this easily accessible information, it is not unreasonable to say that Mr. Bush *fabricated*, or *grossly exaggerated* known facts while beating the drum for his war. Nonetheless, a lie by any other name is still a lie."

"Objection overruled," Hurst-Brown answered. "Mr. McBride, you may continue."

"Thank you, Your Honor. We pick up with Mr. Bush's comments to a third group of congressmen on September 26, 2002. He said, 'It is clear Saddam has weapons of mass destruction: anthrax, VX and still needs plutonium, and he has not been shy about trying to find it. Time frame to Iraq having a nuke would be six months.'

"Following his White House meetings with selected members of Congress, Mr. Bush engaged in another critical part of his strategy—scaremongering to the American people. In a primetime speech from Cincinnati, October 7, 2002, five months and thirteen days before the war, he said, 'Iraq gathers the most serious dangers of our age in one place. The danger is already significant and it only grows worse with time. Facing clear evidence of peril, we cannot wait for the final proof, the "smoking gun" that could come in the form of a mushroom cloud.' These statements and many others prove conclusively that Mr. Bush engaged in an orchestrated propaganda campaign to brainwash and/or frighten the American people into believing there was a 'clear and present' danger that the United States would be attacked by Iraq. Yet again, there was no truth to what Mr. Bush was telling the American public and the world, as was proven during and after the invasion.

"October 10, 2002, five months and ten days before the war. Based on Mr. Bush's campaign of misinformation and lies, the US House of Representatives passed a resolution authorizing him to use the US armed forces in Iraq, *but only to* 'defend national security.' The resolution stated: 'The president is authorized to use the armed forces of the United States as he determines to be necessary and appropriate in order to *defend the national security of the United States* against the continuing threat posed by Iraq.' Note the resolution said 'defend the national security of the United States.' Let me state the truth clearly for the record. Iraq had *never attacked*, or *threatened to attack*, or even *had the capacity to attack*, the United States. Fear of Iraq attacking America was never a reality. It was drummed up by the accused.

"Early November 2002, four and a half months before the war. Mr. Bush met in the White House with Hans Blix, head of the UN Iraq weapons inspection team. He said, 'You've got to understand, Mr. Blix, you've got the force of the United States behind you. And I'm prepared to use it if need be to enforce this resolution. The decision to go to war will be my decision. Don't ever feel like what you're saying is making the decision.' Your Honors, please note, Mr. Bush said, 'The decision to go to war will be *my decision*.' He was correct in saying that. As president and commander in chief, it was *his* decision.

"Late November 2002, three months and three weeks before the war. UN weapons inspectors began inspections on the ground in Iraq, unopposed by Saddam or any other Iraqis. *Seven hundred and thirty-one inspections took place* between late November 2002 and March 2003, especially in Baghdad, where a surprise search at one of Saddam's presidential palaces yielded nothing. Repeat inspections allowed by Saddam found no WMD or any other offending weaponry.

"January 27, 2003, one month and twenty-two days before the war. A United Nations Security Council report by the director general of the International Atomic Energy Agency, Mohamed ElBaradei, stated, 'We have found no evidence that Iraq has revived its nuclear weapons program since its elimination of the program in the 1990s. We should be able within the next few months to provide credible assurance that Iraq has no nuclear program.'"

McBride turned yet again to the judges. "Your Honors, please take note of this: *Fifty-two days before the invasion*, the International Atomic Energy Agency was saying they *had found no evidence* Saddam had nuclear weapons. But ever anxious for his war, Mr. Bush got desperate.

"February 7, 2003, one month and thirteen days before the war. French president Jacques Chirac called Mr. Bush offering guidance. 'I don't share your spirit for why we need war. War is not inevitable. There are alternative ways to reach our goals.' Mr. Bush responded, 'I view an armed Saddam Hussein as a direct threat to the American people.' In other words, *Bugger off, Mr. Chirac.*

"February 10, 2003, one month and ten days before the war. French president Chirac, German chancellor Gerhard Schröder, and Russian president Vladimir Putin issued a joint statement calling for extended United Nations weapons inspections in Iraq. Chirac stated emphatically, 'Nothing today justifies war. Russia, Germany, and France are determined to ensure that everything possible is done to disarm Iraq peacefully.'

"February 14, 2003, thirty-four days before the war. Hans Blix presented his findings to the UN Security Council, stating 'Since we arrived in Iraq, *we have conducted more than four hundred inspections* covering more than three hundred sites. All inspections were performed without notice and access was almost always provided promptly. More than two hundred chemical and more than one hundred biological samples have been collected and *no prohibited weapons or substances have been found.'* Please note that this was thirty-four days before Mr. Bush ordered the invasion of Iraq, plenty of time for him to have stopped his war, or at least postponed it.

"March 5, 2003, fifteen days before the war. Mr. Bush met with an envoy sent by Pope John Paul II, Cardinal Pio Laghi, whose message was, 'There would be civilian casualties and it would deepen the gulf between the Christian world and the Muslim world. It would not be a just war. It would be illegal and it would not make things better.' Mr. Bush responded, 'Absolutely, it will make things better.'

"March 16, 2003. French president Chirac was interviewed on the highly regarded CBS news program *60 Minutes*, during which he called for UN inspectors in Iraq to be given another thirty days. Later that same day at a press conference, Mr. Bush commented on President Chirac's request for patience, saying, 'It's a delaying tactic.' Then getting desperate he said, 'I'm going to have to give Saddam Hussein an ultimatum. Saddam will have forty-eight hours to get out of Iraq with his sons,' adding, 'We have concluded that tomorrow is a moment of truth for the world. The Iraqi regime will disarm itself, or the Iraqi regime will be resolved by force.'

"March 17, 2003, three days before the war. Mr. Bush met with the National Security Council in the White House. Colin Powell reported that nothing had changed overnight. Mr. Bush warned General Franks over a secure video link that he might have to execute Op Plan 1003 V within forty-eight hours. Later that evening, Mr. Bush made a nationwide address in which he said, 'My fellow citizens, events in Iraq have now reached the final days of decision.'"

McBride addressed the judges. "That was not true, of course. Only those events in his mind had led him to reach a final decision. Mr. Bush went on to say, 'The Iraqi regime has used diplomacy as a ploy to gain time and advantage.' Maybe so, but that was not a legal justification for the United States to wage war on the country. Rogue nations defy UN sanctions all the time and are dealt with accordingly, with rebukes, sanctions, pressure from their allies . . . but not full-on war.

"March 19, 2003—nine a.m. in Washington, DC, five p.m. in Iraq. Mr. Bush asked his National Security Council, 'Do you have any last comments, recommendations, or thoughts?' No one did. Mr. Bush pronounced, 'For the sake of peace in the world and security for our country and the rest of the free world and for the freedom of the Iraqi people, I give Secretary Rumsfeld the order to execute Operation Iraqi Freedom,' thus providing clear and irrefutable evidence once and for all that George W. Bush personally ordered the war in Iraq, and must personally accept the responsibility for the death and damage caused by his war."

McBride turned to address Bush specifically. "There were no winners in your war, Mr. Bush, only losers."

"No winners?" George Bush fired back as he leapt to his feet. He had listened to McBride's litany with little interest, but his last comment was more than he could bear. "Saddam Hussein is a dead man and Iraq has got about thirty-four million people who are no longer living under his tyranny."

Hurst-Brown rapped his gavel with noted force. "Order in the Court."

White grabbed Bush's arm to restrain him, but he wasn't finished with McBride. "You can't just recite a bunch of out-of-context, unfounded comments and expect anybody to take you seriously."

Hurst-Brown had had enough. "Mr. White, either your client shows some respect for these proceedings or we'll find him in contempt of the Court. Do I make myself clear?"

White, knowing he needed to handle the situation quickly or there would be consequences, responded with humility. "Apologies, Your Honors. These were difficult times, and people still have strong opinions and even stronger emotions. Respectfully, we apologize to the Court."

Hurst-Brown replied, "Apology accepted, Mr. White, but ensure it doesn't happen again. Mr. McBride, you may continue."

McBride pressed on. "March 20, 2003. Teams of US Special Operations Forces entered Iraq. The Iraq War had begun. One year, five and a half months after George Bush started his drumbeat for war, he got his war.

"Before moving on, I want to clearly define and emphasize the magnitude of George Bush's distortion of the truth. Following his war, the Center for Public Integrity stated, 'It is beyond dispute that *Iraq did not possess any weapons of mass destruction or have meaningful ties to al Qaeda.*' The report listed nine hundred and thirty-five false statements made by Mr. Bush and his closest aides regarding the security risk posed by Iraq during the time following the attacks of 9/11, and leading up to the Iraq War in March of 2003. While we have entered into evidence some of the more obvious testimony, the report confirms that Mr. Bush personally made *two hundred and thirty-two false statements* about Iraq and Saddam Hussein, and *twenty-eight false statements about Iraq's links to al Qaeda.* As a direct result of Mr. Bush's campaign of lies, scaremongering and warmongering, an assault force of two hundred and fifty thousand US and coalition forces invaded the sovereign country of Iraq."

McBride addressed the judges directly. "Your Honors, on this very day of shame, George Bush addressed the American people live on prime-time television. He looked straight into the camera and said, 'American and coalition forces are in early stages of military operations to disarm Iraq.' Of what? No one had found any WMD because there weren't any. Mr. Bush maintained that he was doing this 'to free its people' without having the slightest idea of what to do with the Iraqi people once Saddam had been removed, which created a monumental problem that plagues the world to this day. He concluded that his aim was 'to defend the world from grave danger.' Defend the world from *grave danger*— in Iraq? Saddam Hussein was so neutered by this time that he wasn't even a threat to his own people, much less the people of the world. George Bush, for whatever distorted, convoluted, sick, and disastrous reasons, had it all wrong."

McBride, hoping to preempt an objection from the defense, turned quickly to the defendant. "Mr. Bush, your war created an enormous amount of anger around the world, leading to huge protests in six hundred cities, among them three million protesters in Rome, one million in London, and hundreds of thousands in New York City and Paris. This worldwide protest of your war was the largest global protest event in human history."

With increasing theatricality, McBride turned back to the judges. "Your Honors, it is a fundamental principle of international law that states are prohibited from using military force except in self-defense, or unless its use is formally authorized by the UN Security Council. Quite obviously the United States did not act in self-defense, because Iraq didn't invade it, or have any intention or capacity of invading. And not only did the United States *not* have authorization from the Security Council, but by a vote of eleven to four the Security Council specifically opposed military action. The only reason George Bush took it upon himself to wage war against Iraq was to seek personal revenge against Saddam Hussein.

"And so we can see and understand the facts, and thus know the truth. The evidence is chronological, plentiful, clear, and conclusive. This man sitting before you, George W. Bush, is the single person most responsible for causing the Iraq War. It all started with him. It could never have happened without him. And now he must accept the responsibility for the death and destruction resulting from his war. Following the 9/11 attacks, he used his nation's emotional wounds and desire for revenge to attack Iraq and topple Saddam Hussein—instead of taking out Osama bin Laden and al Qaeda. Other than Hitler's action in connection with World War II, the ICC may never have such a clear-cut, open-and-shut case against a single perpetrator of such horrific, destructive, unnecessary and illegal war crimes than this man, George Bush.

"Your Honors, I pray for the peoples of Iraq, indeed all the peoples of the world, that you see the Iraq War for what it was, and this man for what he did. If leaders of superpowers are allowed to wage unnecessary and illegal wars with impunity, humankind is doomed to experience more such disastrous wars in the future.

"That said, George Bush couldn't and didn't do it alone. Your Honors, as is well known, the ICC first seeks to bring to justice *the one person most responsible* for causing the crime or crimes to occur. It also provides that each coconspirator must stand trial for his or her role in the commission of these crimes. We want to make abundantly clear that George Bush's coconspirators in the creation and waging of the Iraq War, including Vice President Dick Cheney, National Security Advisor Condoleezza Rice, Secretary of Defense Donald Rumsfeld, and Deputy Secretary of Defense Paul Wolfowitz, will be the focus of further investigations, and if warranted, prosecution."

McBride paused to let his comments linger in the Court. No one spoke. No one moved.

Finally, McBride concluded simply, "Your Honors, the prosecution rests."

Judge Miyako Kimura responded, "Thank you, Mr. McBride. At this time the Court will take a twenty-minute break after which we invite defense counsel to offer its opening statement on behalf of the accused."

No clear-thinking person in or outside of the United States would conclude that America would simply stand by idly while a former president was tried for war crimes at the ICC. The

United States insisted that an emergency meeting of the per-manent members of the UN Security Council—China, France, Russia, the United Kingdom, and the United States—be called. Following much heated debate, the majority vote was to not have the UN override the jurisdiction of the ICC relative to the administration of international law. The Bush trial would continue.

The United States had to come to terms with the fact that whatever it did, it would do unilaterally, and without the sup-port of its traditional allies. Following the failed attempt by the Special Operations Forces to rescue Mr. Bush, the US military brass moved to Plan B: move one of its supercarriers, ironically but not surprisingly the USS *George H. W. Bush*, into the hostile theater.

The USS *Bush*, named of course after the forty-first president, was built in 2009 at a cost of 6.2 billion dollars, and was well equipped with ninety fixed-wing aircraft and an assortment of helicopters.

It was only fitting that the US Navy would name this mag-nificent battleship after George H. W. Bush, who, at the age of eighteen became the youngest officer to receive his Naval Aviator Wings and Naval Commission. He was also awarded the Distinguished Flying Cross and three Air Medals for cou-rageous service in the Pacific Theater.

When the order was given, the USS *Bush* was patrolling the coasts of Turkey and Syria in the eastern waters of the Mediterranean Sea. Traveling at speeds in excess of thirty knots, she made her way west across the Mediterranean, turned north at the Atlantic Ocean, traveled through the English Channel, and arrived at her destination in the North Sea, within clear eyesight of The Hague and within a few miles of the ICC.

Of course the unannounced arrival of a US battleship off the coast of The Hague caught the attention of everybody in and following the case—precisely what it was meant to do. Since the Americans didn't ask permission, and weren't announcing their intentions, all opinions were merely speculation. Some journalists theorized that the US military would not tolerate a guilty verdict from the ICC and would launch a massive rescue attempt of Mr. Bush in response. Others observed that George Bush waged the Iraq War, and battleship or no battleship, if that was found to be criminal under international law, then so be it.

Proceeding with business, all were assembled back in the ICC courtroom following the break. After being called by Judge Kimura, Ed White smiled confidently at Bush as he stood to make the opening statement for the defense. "Thank you, Your Honor. First, and let me be clear about this: What the International Criminal Court has done, and is doing to a former president of the United States is placing its very existence in jeopardy. Article 55(2) of your Rome Statute requires a person being arrested to be informed of the basis for their arrest, their right to remain silent, without such silence being considered as guilt or innocence, and the right to counsel—essentially the equivalent of America's Miranda warning. Your commandos just scooped Mr. Bush up off a golf course and deposited him into your custody. Anyone who knows international law is aware that the 'bounty hunter' technique used to abduct the defendant, along with failing to properly inform him of his rights, is not only reprehensible in and of itself, but serves to prejudice the case.

"Furthermore, as a legal precedent, it should be noted that American presidents in the twentieth century alone have waged wars in Korea, Vietnam, and Kuwait, and have done so with impunity. The US Constitution makes it the job of the president to protect the Republic, and Mr. Bush, like all presidents before him, was doing his constitutionally mandated job.

"Moreover, international law is based entirely on consent, and the United States has signed no document recognizing the ICC's power over its citizens.

"Thus based on the lack of judicial authority, illegal kidnaping of the defendant, and failure to notify him of his rights; defense moves for dismissal of this case, and the immediate release of former president Bush, at which time we will escort him back to America."

The courtroom reacted with stunned surprise.

McBride leapt to his feet, "Objection, Your Honor. This is nothing more than blatant disregard and disrespect for this Court of international justice."

Judge Hurst-Brown took the lead. "Objection noted. Mr. McBride, please be seated." McBride hesitated a beat too long. "Your objection is noted. Now, sit down."

He did.

Hurst-Brown turned his attention back to the lead defense attorney. "Now, Mr. White, about your request. Up until now the ICC has relied upon member states and their traditional police forces to effectuate its arrest warrants. The military operation used in this case departs from that practice, and you are correct to raise the point. However, most courts, and indeed American courts after the Supreme Court decision in *Alvarez-Machain*, do not question how criminal defendants come before them when arriving from abroad. Moreover, Article 55 only deals with questioning during the investigation phase, not the actual arrest. Consequently, your motion is denied. Any further comments or questions?"

White responded. "Yes. We have a lot more to ask and say, Your Honor, but respectfully, the defense requests a continuance until tomorrow afternoon."

"Very well, Mr. White. Request granted." Hurst-Brown pronounced after getting visual approval from his fellow judges. "*The Prosecutor v. George W. Bush* is adjourned until fourteen hundred hours tomorrow."

CHAPTER EIGHT

Eye of the Storm

*Our chief want is someone who will inspire us
to be what we know we could be.*
—Ralph Waldo Emerson

The Hague was deemed to be the international city of peace and justice when it hosted the world's first peace conference in 1899. In the early twentieth century, the Scottish American millionaire Andrew Carnegie built the Peace Palace to house the Permanent Court of Arbitration. It was no surprise that when the United Nations sought a city to be the home of the International Criminal Court, The Hague was the de facto choice.

It was here in The Hague that Mrs. George W. Bush, the former first lady of the United States, arrived after a long but uneventful journey. Starting in Crawford, Texas, a convoy of Secret Service officers loaded Mrs. Bush and her luggage into a black SUV and transported her to a nearby airport, where she boarded a US government Gulfstream jet for a flight to Washington, DC. At Dulles Airport she was hustled onto a KLM flight bound nonstop for Amsterdam. For privacy and security reasons, the State Department had taken over the entire first-class cabin, having displaced other passengers to either business class or later flights. Mrs. Bush settled into seat 1A with two Secret Service officers and two Special Ops Marines seated in the last rows. After a pleasant but mostly uneaten dinner, she closed her eyes for what would understandably be a fitful night's sleep.

Laura Bush was born Laura Lane Welch, the child of Harold and Jenna Welch, on November 4, 1946, in the boom-or-bust town of Midland, Texas. Her father served his country valiantly as a member of the 105th Army Battalion, which liberated the German town of Nordhausen, site of the Mittelbau-Dora concentration camp, housing five thousand prisoners.

Laura graduated from Southern Methodist University in Dallas and then the University of Texas in Austin, where she earned her master's degree in library science. She returned home to Midland to work as a school librarian until she met and married George Bush in 1977. Although he was raised as an Episcopalian, George converted to Laura's Methodist faith and they were married in the First Methodist Church.

When Laura arrived in The Hague, she checked into Hotel Des Indes, an old world hostelry considered one of the best in the city, dropped off her luggage, and, along with a suitcase full of her husband's clothes and accessories, was whisked off to the ICC Detention Centre.

Mr. Bush was pacing around a table in the middle of a meeting room when the door opened and Laura entered. According to close friends who knew the Bushes well, a long welcoming hug was followed by many questions: How are you doing? What happened? Can the ICC do this?

Next they talked about their twin daughters, Barbara and Jenna (named after their grandmothers, Barbara Bush and Jenna Welch).

At last, Laura voiced the all-important question. "How's the trial going?"

"It's going . . . that's the first problem."

"Meaning?"

"Meaning I never should've been brought here in the first place."

"Couldn't Ed White get you out of this mess?"

"He tried."

"And?"

"I'm still here."

"George, there has to be something we can do."

"Honestly, Laura, we *are* doing everything we can. I got a great team of lawyers and justice is on our side. There's no way any rational court in the world could find me guilty of war crimes."

"Including the ICC?"

"Including the ICC."

Laura studied her husband's eyes. "I pray to God you're right."

Their conversation eventually turned to an incident that occurred in April 2001 when British prime minister Tony Blair and his wife, Cherie, were visiting the Bushes at their ranch in Crawford, Texas. Mrs. Blair used the occasion to plead with Mr. Bush to reconsider his opposition to the International Criminal Court, and to take the necessary steps to have the United States rejoin. After all, she argued, Great Britain, France, Canada, and other powerful allies of the United States were members; why not the United States? Nonetheless, Mr. Bush dismissed Mrs. Blair's plea.

Not having forgotten that conversation, Laura wondered aloud, "George, would we be sitting here today if you didn't have the United States resign its membership of the ICC?"

Mr. Bush considered the question for a moment and answered, "No, it may have happened even sooner. Let's not forget, the UK is a member of the ICC and the Brits leveled charges against Tony Blair in English courts."

After an hour, per ICC protocol, the meeting of George and Laura Bush came to an end. Laura lifted a Bible from her purse, and opened it to a preselected passage. "Here, darling, we should read this."

George took the book, shared a loving moment with his wife, and read in a solemn voice: "Proverbs 3:33. The curse of the Lord is on the house of the wicked, but he blesses the home of the just. Surely he scorns the scornful, but gives grace to the humble. The wise shall inherit glory, but shame shall be the legacy of fools."

The Hague features pleasant walks, interesting smallish boutiques and hotels, and a collection of inviting watering holes that provide food and drink for the many internationals who work at the ICC. One of the most popular is Paraplu—Dutch for "umbrella." Michael McBride and Nadia Shadid sat in the back corner of the restaurant picking at bites of roasted lamb and sipping a French burgundy. Nadia broke a lingering silence by saying softly, "The tragedy of this, of course, is that we shouldn't be having this trial."

Michael cocked his head indicating he wasn't quite sure what she was talking about. "Meaning?"

"There shouldn't have been a war in the first place. Iraq is another Vietnam. What is it about America—or at least some Americans—that makes them want to enforce democracy on other countries that do not want it? Vietnam, Iraq, what's next?"

Michael took a swig of wine while considering the questions. "I don't have a suitable answer for your first question, and as for your second question—all sane Americans should do everything in their power to oppose the war machine, and ensure there are no more Vietnams or Iraqs."

"A second tragedy is that my country was punished way out of proportion to what Saddam may or may not have been doing at the time."

"He sure had done plenty of horrible things in the past, but yeah . . . what was *he actually doing at the time* to deserve that war?"

"Ironically, he was writing his fourth book. The English translation would be: *Get Out of Here, Curse You!* He finished it two days before the US invasion."

Michael's look revealed he was not aware of that. Nadia added, "It's incredible that a country with the rich heritage of Iraq could fall into such modern-day despair."

Michael felt a profound sadness for Nadia—for all Iraqi people. "My sincere hope is that one day your country will return to its former glory."

"A noble wish devoutly to be desired, however unlikely it might be."

CHAPTER NINE

Dueling Barristers

*What good fortune for governments
that men do not think.*

—Adolf Hitler

L ate autumn had turned to early winter in The Hague. Leaves
were gone. Cold, wet weather was forecast. Mittens, scarves,
and hats appeared.

The nonstop gavel-to-gavel live streaming of *The Prosecutor v.
George W. Bush* had been very well received by audiences around
the world. So, in a next-generation attempt by the ICC to be
even more transparent, the ICC came up with something entirely
new in the world of jurisprudence—perhaps even revolutionary.
It commissioned the installation of three huge monitors, thirty
meters high by twenty meters long, for public viewing outside
the ICC buildings. These monitors were placed at strategic loca-
tions to service those who could not gain access to the public
gallery inside. Both public and press likened the monitors to
those outside Centre Court at Wimbledon, or inside a popular
rock concert. International criminal law had gone high-tech and
mainstream.

At 14:00 CET the following day, the Court readjourned for day three of the Bush trial. Outside, thousands were gathering to watch the trial for the first time on the new large-screen monitors. Inside, the public gallery was packed to the gills as usual. But on this occasion, the audience included an American woman much camouflaged but unmistakably Mrs. George W. Bush. In the crowded courtroom, the clerk gave the command, "All rise." All did except George Bush and his defense team. Three ICC judges entered and sat. Others sat as well.

Presiding judge Harrison Hurst-Brown began the day's proceeding. "The International Criminal Court is now in session: *The Prosecutor v. George W. Bush.* Defense counsel, you may continue with your opening statement."

Lead defense attorney Edward White, dressed more fashionably than usual in a gray suit with contrasting pink tie, restarted his defense. "Thank you, Your Honor. Good day, everybody. Ironclad evidence in the intelligence business is scarce. Experienced weapons analysts are often forced to make 'informed judgments.' During the period before the Iraq War, evidence regarding Iraq's military capacity was confusing and contradictory.

"It is factually true that no one found definitive proof that Iraq had biological weapons or weapons of mass destruction. Yet, coupled with the incontrovertible proof that Saddam Hussein *had such weapons* in the past . . . a conclusion that he still had them seemed obvious, especially as he was a notorious liar, manipulator, criminal, and cheat. The alternative view was that Saddam didn't have such weapons. But to arrive at that conclusion, much accumulated intelligence would have to be ignored. The most sensible conclusion was that he *probably had* WMD, and who in their right mind would dare to bet he didn't?

"Putting the evidence or lack of evidence aside, there were many reasons why George Bush had justification for the Iraq War. Among them were: first, to resolve certain unanswered questions left after the first Bush administration, when, in 1991 after the Gulf War, it let Saddam Hussein consolidate power and slaughter opponents; second, to protect America's closest ally in the region, Israel, and to improve its strategic position by eliminating a hostile enemy; third, to permit the withdrawal of US forces from Saudi Arabia, where they had been stationed for decades; fourth, to quiet anti-American rhetoric that threatened America's allies in the region; fifth, to create another source of oil for the US market, namely, Iraq, and thus reduce dependency on oil from Saudi Arabia; sixth, to help transition an important Middle Eastern country ruled by a ruthless dictator into a pro-American democracy capable, in time, of functioning under free elections and the rule of law; seventh, to create a democracy in the region that could serve as a model to other friendly Arab states, notably Egypt and Saudi Arabia; and finally and perhaps most importantly, eighth, to protect and defend the American people both at home and abroad in this new era of global terrorism.

"So upon fair and dispassionate analysis, Mr. Bush would not have been fulfilling his obligations to protect and defend the United States of America, and other friendly countries around the world, if he had not gone to war with Iraq."

Gaining momentum, White turned to address the ICC judges. "However much the ICC considers its legal imperative to protect the citizens of the world, I assure it that the president of the United States considers his constitutional imperative to protect his own citizens of equal importance. Under international humanitarian law—and the Rome Statute itself, for that matter—the death of civilians during an armed conflict, no matter how grave and regrettable, does not in and of itself constitute a war crime. International law permits an opposing country to carry out proportional attacks against military objectives, even when it is known that some civilian deaths or injuries will occur. A crime occurs only if there is an *intentional attack directed against a civilian population*. Such was definitely *not* the case in the Iraq War.

"Moreover, there are many fundamental principles of international criminal law that, when considered individually and collectively, expressly preclude the trying of this case against former president Bush. While all crimes within the jurisdiction of the Court would seem to be grave, the Rome Statute requires an additional threshold of 'gravity' for war crimes, as set forth in Article 8(1), which states that 'the Court shall have jurisdiction in respect of war crimes in particular when committed as part of a plan or policy or as part of a *large-scale commission* of such crimes.'

"Informed people familiar with this case know the Iraq War was not, and was never intended to be, a large-scale invasion of the country. Defense will prove that this criterion for war crimes *is not satisfied* in this case. However, even if one were to assume that Article 8(1) had been satisfied, it would then be necessary to consider the messy issues of jurisdiction, admissibility, the rule of complementarity, and other legal matters attendant to this case.

"Furthermore, Article 8(2) criminalizes an attack by an opposing nation only in the knowledge that such an attack will cause incidental loss of life or injury to civilians, damage to civilian objects, or widespread and severe damage to the natural environment that would be *clearly excessive in relation to the direct overall military advantage anticipated*. Available evidence does establish that civilians died or were injured during the subject military operations. But such information does not indicate coalition forces specifically attacked the civilian population, or that they were clearly excessive in relation to the military advantage gained.

"All available evidence is to be measured by the existence of information that monitored excessiveness in relation to military advantage gained. Publicly available information from the United States and the United Kingdom provides evidence of compliance to the above, as follows: First, a list of potential targets were identified in advance; second, commanders had legal advice available to them at all times and were made aware of the need to comply with international humanitarian law including the principles of proportionality; third, detailed computer modeling was used in assessing targets; fourth, political, legal, and military oversight was established for target approval; and fifth, real-time targeting information, including collateral damage assessment, was communicated by the two headquarters.

"This information has not been contradicted by any source and thus perforce must be taken into consideration in accordance with customary legal evaluation. The defense will prove conclusively that approximately 85 percent of the weapons used by coalition aircraft were precision guided, which confirms the effort to minimize casualties. Thus the available information *does not allow* for the conclusion that a clearly excessive crime within the jurisdiction of the Court has been committed.

"And finally, the United States and the United Kingdom were joined by thirty-eight other countries from around the world which participated in the Iraq War effort. Would it be the intention of the ICC to hold accountable all the leaders of all those countries? If the leaders of forty countries believed the Iraq War was a justifiable war, how can the International Criminal Court decide it was not? Thank you, Your Honors. The defense rests."

Ed White nodded at George Bush as he sat.

The prosecution couldn't risk inaction after the defense had gained such critical ground. After exchanging looks and nods with McBride, Nadia Shadid addressed the judges. "Your Honors, the prosecution requests permission to respond."

"Permission granted," answered Hurst-Brown.

"Thank you, Your Honor." Shadid went on the counterattack. "While the defense puts forth an interesting linguistic argument, it isn't consistent with the facts. The defense contends that the Iraq War was never intended to be 'a large-scale invasion.' That is in total contradiction to the truth. American-led coalition forces waged a full-scale war using massive military force that was described by many as 'shock and awe.' More than three hundred thousand troops were used, and the United States spent *more than a billion dollars a day* fighting that war. Anybody who knows the facts could only describe it as *a large-scale invasion.* As a result, Iraq was defeated within months—weeks, really.

"Next point: The prosecution pleads that the Court *reject* the defense's use of Article 8(2), which states that civilian casualties are acceptable in light of the military advantage gained. War crimes, as defined in international law, are committed if the perpetrator is responsible for the killing of *even one person.* Mr. Bush's war caused the deaths of approximately six hundred and fifty thousand human beings, as reported in the respected British medical journal *The Lancet.*

"As to 'military advantage gained' . . . *What military advantage was gained?* World War II was fought to stop the spread of Hitler's Nazi regime in Russia and Europe. The Vietnam War was fought to address the Western world's fear of communism spreading in Asia—'the domino theory' as it was called. Iraq wasn't trying to spread its ideology, even if it had one. It was only trying to maintain its sovereignty in the contentious Middle East, which took constant diligence. Following the Gulf War that ended in 1991, containment, sanctions, and inspections eliminated Saddam's ability to threaten other countries, most certainly including the United States. The truth is that fighting the Iraq War meant America was noticeably *more disadvantaged than advantaged*, because it had to take responsibility for a damaged country that it damaged even more.

"What the defense counsel refuses to take responsibility for is George Bush causing the war to happen in the first place and recognizing the tremendous carnage in terms of military and civilian lives lost, and physical structures destroyed as a result of his war.

"George Bush's stated goals for waging his war were first to remove WMD, of which there were none. Then it was to protect America from an attack by Iraq. As has been proven, Saddam had no interest in or capacity to attack America. As a reminder, and for the record, Saddam Hussein was once an ally of the United States. In the early 1980s, Iran's shah was overthrown by the Ayatollah Khomeini, which led to the Iran-Iraq War. Saddam invaded Iran with the support of Arab states, Europe, and the United States, all of which provided funding and military equipment. Saddam was regarded as *the defender of the Arab world*. Nonetheless, with absolutely no justification for attacking Iraq and toppling Saddam, and all the justification in the world for finding and killing bin Laden and destroying al Qaeda, George Bush started his war with Iraq. Even his brother Jeb Bush, while campaigning for the presidency in 2015, said, 'Based on what we now know, I wouldn't have gone in. It was a mistake.'

"The facts prove that George Bush was repeatedly given relevant and accurate information, and yet he chose to ignore it. It is literally impossible for him to have gone into his office at the White House and dealt with the people he interacted with on a daily basis and not have known this information. The truth is, he knew these facts during the entire buildup to the war and chose to ignore them because *the truth did not serve his agenda.* He spread false information that supported his war, so he could gain the approval necessary to wage his war. Why didn't he just find and kill Osama bin Laden and thus satisfy America's public thirst for the revenge of 9/11? It should be noted that after Mr. Bush left office, in May of 2011, President Barack Obama ordered an attack in which sixteen Navy SEALs entered a house in Abbottabad, Pakistan, and *in fifteen minutes found and killed Osama bin Laden,* after which they departed with his body to bury him at sea. The entire operation took forty-two minutes.

"There are possible other motivations for George Bush's war. A war would stimulate the US economy and satisfy his voter base—note that he easily won his second-term election. A war would protect Israel. A war would avenge the assassination attempt on his father. It would protect US allies' oil interest in Iraq and the region. The fact is we may never know exactly why George Bush started his war, unless he decides to tell us. But wage his war he did, and now he must bear the responsibility for the consequences of that war."

In full flow and at the top of her game, Shadid walked confidently toward the judges and continued. "Your Honors, the prosecution would like to engage in a little housekeeping and address some legal rudiments at this time. Article 30 of the Rome Statute provides that a person shall be criminally responsible and liable for punishment for a crime within the jurisdiction of the

Court only if the material elements are *committed with intent and knowledge*. Existence of intent and knowledge are confirmed by actual facts. The prosecution has proven that the defendant had clear and abundant 'intent and knowledge' before and during the Iraq War. Thank you, Your Honors. The prosecution rests."

"Thank you, Ms. Shadid. Does defense counsel wish to refute the prosecution's assertions?"

Ed White responded quickly, "No, Your Honor. We will let the facts speak for themselves."

"Thank you, sir," Hurst-Brown said and rapped his gavel. "Court is adjourned until oh nine hundred hours tomorrow at which time the prosecution may commence with witness testimony."

CHAPTER TEN

Parade of Prosecution Witnesses

In a time of universal deceit, telling the truth
is a revolutionary act.
—Anonymous

The case of *The Prosecutor v. George W. Bush* had taken on such universal importance that coverage of the trial was reported by all manner of news organizations around the world and beamed up to astronauts circling the globe. Major outdoor stadiums and indoor arenas put the contiguous live feed on their huge monitors and, even though they didn't charge for admission, by the time they did charge for parking and concessions, everybody seemed pleased. However, no public viewing of the trial could match what happened in, of all places, North Korea.

The trial of George W. Bush in The Hague had ironically caught the particular fancy of North Korean dictator Kim Jong Un. Unable to resist the theater of a former president of the United States on trial for war crimes, he mandated that coverage of the event be made available at the Rungrado Stadium in

Pyongyang, famously the largest stadium in the world, seating one hundred and fifty thousand people.

The venue was ordinarily used for sporting, civic, and political events of both national and international importance, such as the entertainment spectacle produced in 2000 for visiting US secretary of state under then president Bill Clinton, Madeleine Albright. Of only marginally less importance, the stadium was also used for public viewing of the execution of North Korean army generals who were implicated in a 1990 attempted assassination of Kim Jong Il, all of whom were summarily put to death by burning.

While the stadium did have some capacity for large-screen viewing, Kim Jong Un determined that more needed to be done for George W. Bush's trial. In a rare showing of joint Korean cooperation, a request went out to a South Korean electronics company well-known for its ability to create huge screens for movie theaters inside and mass public viewing outside. In an almost unbelievably short amount of time, multiple jumbo screens were installed in the stadium, and the live feed of the Bush trial was projected onto the screens, translated into Korean, and thus made available for one and all to see, free of charge, on a daily basis.

The following morning at nine o'clock CET sharp, the usual assemblage was present in the ICC courtroom, along with several witnesses brought by both the prosecution and defense to provide testimony. After presiding judge Hurst-Brown gaveled the trial into session, co–prosecuting attorney Nadia Shadid began. "Good morning, Your Honors. The prosecution would like to state that it will present an abundance of witness testimony along with US government statistics that further proves beyond any lingering doubt that hundreds of thousands of American, Iraqi, and coalition soldiers were killed in George Bush's war.

"To begin, we wish to call the Court's attention to Prosecution Evidence #3." Per standard courtroom procedure, the ICC judges, the defense team, and all others in the courtroom and public gallery looked at the monitors or referred to the binders of evidence provided.

Shadid continued, "This document, according to US military intelligence sources, is *a complete list of all American soldiers who lost their lives in the Iraq War.* Included are the name, picture, hometown, military rank, age, and date of death of each of the deceased. The list is presented in chronological order from the first American soldier to die—Jonathan Lee Gifford, age thirty, of Decatur, Illinois, who was killed in action March 23, three days after the war began—to the last American soldier to die, David Emmanuel Hickman, age twenty-three, from Greensboro, North Carolina, who died November 14, 2011.

"Your Honors, as mothers, fathers, wives, husbands, siblings, and friends of these fallen soldiers have had to relate and relive their emotional pain so many times already, we will provide a measured amount of testimony regarding military deaths. Every bit as important as the American and Iraqi casualties suffered in the war is the experience of the Iraqi people during the war. It is in this context, Your Honors, that I request permission to approach the bench."

Hurst-Brown granted permission, and Shadid approached the bench. Seeing this, co-defense attorney Meredith Lott approached the bench as well.

The two opposing female attorneys exchanged brief but hostile looks before Shadid began in a quiet voice, "Your Honors, the prosecution's first witness is a woman from Iraq who became a somewhat famous blogger during the Iraq War. She has agreed to testify under the condition that her identity be kept secret, as she wishes to remain outside the public view for the safety and security of herself and her family. She is here at the ICC but will testify only if she can wear a burka, have her voice distorted, and use the name under which she published her blog. Her testimony is critical to the prosecution's case and we plead for approval from the Court to proceed with this witness."

Lott countered, "Your Honors, we strongly object. Our client has the right to know the identity of his accusers and to contest the evidence given against him. How can we do so if we don't even know her real identity and can't even see her face? Article 67 of the Rome Statute guarantees these rights in a fair trial."

"Maybe so," Shadid responded, "but Article 68 empowers the Court to protect witnesses who may be in danger of retaliation for cooperating with the Court. Keeping this witness's identity secret is critical to her safety."

Lott countered again, "This is exactly why the ICC had black curtains installed over the public gallery windows. Just draw the curtains closed and disallow the burka. At least we'll be able to see who she is."

"Your Honors, please do not forget the overriding issue of transparency and public interest in this trial. If we close the curtains, the ICC will seem to be operating in secret, which will undermine its legitimacy as an institution. By letting our witness wear her burka, she remains concealed without the Court having to hide the trial from the world."

"But, Your Honors," Lott interjected, "our client's rights are more important than the public's right to view the trial."

After consulting sotto voce with her fellow judges, Judge Miyako Kimura informed the opposing attorneys of the Court's decision. "You both raise valid points. However, on balance, we believe that keeping this trial public and transparent supersedes the defense's need to see this witness's face and best serves the ends of justice. Ms. Shadid, if your witness refers to her blogs, will you make them available to the Court?"

"Yes, Your Honors, we will."

"Then permission is granted."

"Thank you, Your Honors."

Ms. Shadid, pleased and anxious to get started, and Ms. Lott, obviously perturbed, ignored each other and returned to their seats.

Shadid called for the first prosecution witness. A woman wearing a burka, with only a narrow slit wide enough to reveal her eyes, was led into the courtroom by UN guards. As the woman entered, she stopped, looked around the room, and settled her gaze on George Bush. No one spoke. The Iraqi woman continued staring at Bush. When he looked away, she proceeded to the witness bench and sat.

Shadid began by first addressing the judges. "Your Honors, as you no doubt know, there is a very important statement written on a wall in the lobby of this building which says volumes about the ICC. For those of you who do not know, it reads, 'True justice is achieved when voices of victims are heard and their suffering is addressed.' Here at the ICC, for the first time in the history of international criminal justice, victims have the right to participate in proceedings and request reparations. This means they may not only testify, but can also present their views and concerns. This woman contacted the prosecution and asked to testify. We were pleased to accept her offer."

Shadid turned back to the woman and smiled warmly. "Thank you for your bravery. Please know that your voice will be distorted here in the courtroom, on all public showings, and on all other recordings made of your testimony. First, to comply with ICC regulations, all witnesses must read the swearing-in document. Would you please do so now?"

The woman read softly into a microphone, the audio from which was heard in garbled tones throughout the courtroom and the rest of the world, "I solemnly declare that I will speak the truth, the whole truth, and nothing but the truth."

"Thank you. The Court has agreed that we can refer to you as 'Riverbend,' the pen name you used for your blog. Other than your name, would you please introduce yourself?"

"I am female. I am Iraqi. Now I am thirty-nine. When I started writing my blog months after the US invasion of my country, I was twenty-four. I survived the war. That's all you need to know. That's all that matters."

"Why did you start writing your blog?"

"Because I became convinced that George Bush had determined to go to war against Saddam well before 9/11, even though all his claims about weapons of mass destruction were proven to be false, as most Iraqis knew they would be. George Bush's war was based on inaccurate and dishonest reasons. After he declared 'mission accomplished' on May 2, 2003—one and a half months into the war—his war was no longer a war; it became an occupation.

"At first, some Iraqis welcomed the American conquest; some did not. The occupation was first awkward and then quickly became stupid and criminal. The United States never gained enough control to restore any sort of order. Regardless of the enthusiasm some Iraqis initially had for the war, the ongoing support and cooperation from coalition forces that was expected by Iraqis on the street never happened."

Shadid prodded her gently: "Your first blog was posted on August 17, 2003, almost five months to the day after the US invasion."

"Yes. I wanted to start earlier, but I thought, 'Who will read it?' Over time I figured I had nothing to lose. I warned people in my first blog to expect a lot of complaining and ranting."

"And you have some of your blogs with you?"

"Yes. As these events happened years ago, I thought reading my blog would be better than speaking from memory."

"We know you experienced firsthand the death of many friends, friends of friends, and family. May we call your attention to your blog of August 19, 2003? Would you please read from that entry?"

Riverbend flipped through a printout of her blogs, came upon the correct page, and began to read. "Today a child was killed. His name was Omar Jassim, and he was no more than ten years old, maybe eleven. Does anyone hear that? Do they show that on Fox News or CNN? He was killed during an American raid. No one knows why. His family is devastated. Nothing was taken from the house because nothing was found. But the truth is the raids only accomplish one thing: They act as a constant reminder that we are under occupation. We are not free. We are not liberated. We are no longer safe in our homes. Everything now belongs to someone else. I can't see the future at this point, or maybe I don't choose to see it. We're living in this moment with a future we are afraid to contemplate. It's like trying to find your way out of a nightmare. I just wish the Americans would take the oil and go."

Shadid's questions came with more urgency. "We move to the very next day. The UN headquarters in Baghdad is bombed. Twenty-two people are killed. Among the dead is UN special envoy Sergio de Mello, an able diplomat highly respected and regarded by both sides, and widely viewed as the one man who might be able to blend together the complex politics of war-torn Iraq. Would you please read from your blog of August 20, 2003?"

Riverbend nodded and read, "Sergio de Mello's death was a catastrophe. In spite of the fact that the UN was futile in stopping the war, seeing someone like de Mello gave Iraqis some sort of weak hope. It gave you the feeling that, no, Americans could not run amok in Baghdad without the watchful eye of the international community. America, as an occupying power, is responsible for the safety and security of what is left of this country. They have been shirking their duties horribly. I'm terrified. If de Mello could not be kept safe, what's going to happen to the millions of people fearing for their lives in Iraq?"

Shadid allowed for a moment of silent reflection and then continued. "On November 27, 2003, President George Bush visited Baghdad. It was the subject of one of your blogs."

"Yes, he landed at Baghdad International Airport, but don't let the name fool you. It's about twenty miles outside of town. No one is allowed to go near the area. He was gone before any of us knew he had even arrived."

The Iraqi woman looked up from her blog, locked eyes with Bush, and spoke directly to him. "Why did you do that? Why did you sneak in and out of Iraq with such secrecy? Why did you not walk the streets of the country you said you *liberated*?" She stared intently at the former president for many seconds before he blinked and turned away.

The witness continued reading from her blog: "Bush must be proud today; two more terrorists were shot dead. Actually the two 'terrorists' were sisters, one twelve years old and the other fifteen. They were shot by coalition troops while gathering wood from the field, but nobody bothers to report that. They are two Iraqi girls in their teens who were brutally killed by occupation troops—so what? Bush's covert two-hour visit to the Baghdad International Airport is infinitely more important."

Shadid pressed forward with more urgency. "On February 17, 2004, the *New York Times* published an article entitled 'Arabs in US Raising Money to Back Bush.' Would you read your blog of that day?"

Riverbend took a moment to find the post and continued, "The article was written by Leslie Wayne who knows very little about geography. The article basically states that a substantial sum of money supporting Bush's presidential campaign is coming from affluent Arab Americans who support the war on Iraq. Of the five prominent 'Arabs' the author gives as examples of Bush supporters, two are Iranian and a third is Pakistani. Now, this is highly amusing to an Arab because Pakistanis aren't Arabs. And while Iran is our neighbor, Iranians are, generally speaking, not Arabs. You can confirm that with Iranian bloggers. I just wish all those prominent Americans who supported the war, you know, the ones living in Washington and London who attend state dinners at the White House, would pack their Louis Vuitton bags and bring all that money they are contributing to the 'war-hungry imbecile' in the White House to Iraq or Iran to spread democracy and help 'reconstruct' and 'develop' their countries."

"Would you please go to your blogs of March 2004 and share some of them with us?"

Riverbend flipped through a few pages, stopped at one, and read. "Events in the United States are not helping Bush. David Kay, whom the Bush administration confidently predicted would bring home proof of Saddam's weapons of mass destruction, instead tells a Senate committee *he can't find any evidence of their existence*, and that prewar intelligence was *'almost all wrong.'* Did the United States get bad intelligence or did Bush manipulate the intelligence for his own ends? Meanwhile the insurgency mounts. One hundred Iraqis died in suicide bombings in January. On February 10, fifty-four Iraqi people are killed in a bombing as they apply for work at a police station. The next day forty-seven die in an attack outside the Army recruiting center. The insurgency spreads and becomes more intense. Attacks in Karbala kill over one hundred and wound over three hundred. In a car bombing of a Baghdad hotel, twenty-seven people are killed, forty-one wounded."

"March 20, 2003, was the first day of the war. One year later, you posted a blog."

"Yes," Riverbend said and started to read again. "One year ago on this day, the war started during the early hours of the morning. Now, 365 days later, Baghdad has been reduced to rubble. Our electricity is intermittent at best. There are constant fuel shortages and the streets aren't safe. We are trying to fight against extremism that seems to be upon us like a black wave. We watch with disbelief as American troops roam the streets of our towns and cities and break into our homes. Our government facilities have been burnt to the ground. Fifty percent of the working population is jobless and hungry. The streets are dirty and overflowing with sewage. Our jails are fuller than ever with thousands of innocent people. Our homes are being raided and our cars stopped in the streets for inspections. Iraqi journalists are being murdered. Hospitals overflow with patients but are short on everything else: medical supplies, medicine, and doctors. And all the while oil is flowing."

Rereading her blogs made Riverbend angry all over again. She took a deep breath, exhaled slowly, and bowed her head.

Noticing this and wanting to be sure her witness stayed on point, Nadia prodded her to continue. "On April 9, 2004, the provisional government, which you call the Puppet Council, declared the day 'National Day.'"

Riverbend looked up with tears in her eyes. Nadia persisted, "From one Iraqi woman to another, please read your blog of April 9, 2004."

The witness gathered herself and continued. "April 9, 2004; the day the Iraqi puppets called National Day will be marked by us as the day of the Fallujah Massacre. Over three hundred are dead in Fallujah. They are buried in the town football field because no one is allowed near the cemetery. The bodies are decomposing in the heat, and the people are struggling to bury them as quickly as they can. The American statistics don't show the real number of dying Iraqis. They don't show the women and children wounded and bleeding. They don't show the hospitals overflowing with the dead and dying because they don't want to hurt the Americans' feelings."

Riverbend again directed her comments at Bush. "But American people should have seen the human devastation. You, George Bush, you should have seen with your own eyes the price your war had on my people . . . my country."

Bush stared at the woman from Iraq with blank eyes.

Shadid allowed the moment to register with the judges, who sat engrossed in the testimony, and then concluded, "Thank you very much. We have no more questions. Would you like to say anything else?"

"Yes, I would. The American invasion and occupation of Iraq pushed my country into a civil war. A strong Sunni insurgency made security impossible in certain parts of the country. At the same time, Shia leaders with help from Iran pulled together the majority of Shia into a political coalition. With Americans unable to maintain security, it left Iraq disabled, defenseless, and vulnerable. We know what happened after that; Islamic extremists seized the opportunity to use Iraq as a training ground to fight Western influences."

For a final time, the Iraqi witness turned to address her hated enemy. "In case anybody is still wondering how the Islamic State was born and why the renewed hatred of the West came about— you can trace it back to George Bush's war. He claimed he was making the world safe by invading Iraq. In the end, all he did was destroy Iraq and leave the world exposed to terrorism the likes of which it had never seen."

Bush seemed unmoved, dismissive. He glanced over at Ed White, who returned a look of quiet confidence.

Shadid turned to the judges. "Thank you, Your Honors. We have no further questions."

Judge Miyako Kimura said, "Thank you, Ms. Shadid," and turned her attention to the defense. "Does defense counsel wish to cross-examine this witness?"

Meredith Lott stood. "Your Honor, we note for the record that the Court has not provided the defense preparatory information for this witness or offered us the opportunity to meet with her. And since you have decided to also violate your own Rome Statute by determining that the public's view of this trial is more important than our client's rights, we have only seen someone in a burka and cannot possibly gauge this witness's state of mind in order to correctly calibrate our cross-examination. Nonetheless, defense does wish to cross-examine."

"Ms. Lott, the Court notes your objections," Judge Kimura responded. "You may proceed."

"Thank you, Your Honor." Lott smiled at Riverbend and began. "Hello."

Riverbend responded with an icy, "Hello."

"We understand your pen name is 'Riverbend,' but would you please state your actual name in full for the benefit of the Court's records?"

"My actual name is not of consequence. What is of consequence is the content of my message. It was agreed that I could testify under the name I used to write my blog, and that is the name I will use. I wish to remain anonymous so I may continue to write the truth about the residual effects the Iraq War is having on my country without fearing for my safety. I am an Iraqi citizen, a woman, and a Muslim. That should be sufficient."

"Okay 'Riverbend,' we begin. The Muslim religion includes different sects. One's own personal allegiance could well affect one's view of the war, especially as it relates to Saddam Hussein, who was a Sunni Muslim."

Riverbend shot back, "Don't blame the Muslim religion. Every religion has its extremists. In times of chaos and disorder, those extremists flourish. Iraq is full of moderate Muslims who simply believe in the concept 'live and let live.' We get along with each other—Sunnis and Shiites, Muslims, Christians, Jews—we intermarry, we mix and mingle, we live. We build our churches and mosques in the same areas. Our children go to the same school. Religion was never an issue. Next question, if you have one."

"Your selection of blogs was published in a book entitled *Baghdad Burning*, correct?"

"Yes."

"The title itself indicates your view of the war. You know better than me that many Iraqis welcomed that war because it meant the overthrow of Saddam."

"I can promise you fewer Iraqis welcomed that war than George Bush thought or wanted."

"Clearly you're anti-American."

"When I hear 'anti-American,' it angers me. Why does America always identify itself with its military and government? Why does being anti-Bush and antioccupation have to mean a person is anti-American? I am on the side of humanity, freedom, and life, and that's what my book reflects."

"You say you're on the side of 'humanity, freedom, and life.' Thousands of American and coalition soldiers fought and died to free the Iraqi people from the clutches of its evil dictator. Have you no compassion for those lives?"

"There was a time when Iraqi people felt sorry for the troops, regardless of their nationality. We would see them suffering under the Iraqi sun, obviously wishing they were somewhere else, and somehow that vulnerability made them seem less monstrous and more human. But that time passed. Two transitional moments included the destruction of Fallujah and then the notorious photographs of torture at Abu Ghraib prison."

"Thank you, Madam . . . whatever your name is." Lott, obviously realizing she might be doing more damage than good with the cross-examination, turned to address the ICC Judges. "Your Honors, defense rests."

"Thank you, Ms. Lott," Judge Kimura said. Then, turning to Shadid, she asked, "Does the prosecution wish to redirect this witness?"

Shadid answered with a sense of accomplishment, "No, thank you, Your Honor."

"The Court would like to thank the witness from Iraq and wish her a safe journey home."

The woman stood, nodded slightly in the direction of the judges, and was escorted toward the exit by UN guards. As she walked, she purposefully ignored Bush. When she was gone, George Bush lowered his gaze to the floor.

The prosecution called its next witness, Mr. Richard A. Clarke, who read the swearing-in document, after which Ms. Shadid began her questioning. "Mr. Clarke, thank you for joining us today."

Clarke responded in a clear and concise tone. "My pleasure."

"Please state your full name."

"Richard Alan Clarke."

"Born in the United States?"

"Yes. Dorchester, Massachusetts."

"Educated in the United States?"

"Bachelor's degree from the University of Pennsylvania. Master's from the Massachusetts Institute of Technology, among other things."

"Isn't MIT considered to be one of America's finest institutions of learning?"

"Yes."

"As for your diplomatic career, you served under President Ronald Reagan as deputy assistant secretary of state?"

"Yes, for intelligence."

"During the administration of George H. W. Bush you were assistant secretary of state for political-military affairs?"

"Yes."

"During the Clinton administration you were counterterrorism coordinator for the National Security Council?"

"Yes."

"And when President George W. Bush took office you went to work for him. What was your post?"

"National coordinator for security, infrastructure protection, and counterterrorism."

"And your responsibilities were?"

"All matters dealing with terrorism and counterterrorism."

"By the time you worked for George W. Bush, you had served seven presidents in a career spanning thirty years, correct?"

"Yes."

"Would it be accurate to say you were America's foremost authority on terrorism and counterterrorism at that time?"

"Certainly one of the most knowledgeable and experienced."

"George W. Bush was inaugurated January 20, 2001. Only days after the inauguration you requested an urgent meeting. Why?"

"Because we needed to discuss America's greatest threat at the time, al Qaeda and its leader, Osama bin Laden."

"Did your request mention anything about Saddam Hussein or Iraq?"

"No. At that time we judged Saddam and Iraq to be of minimal risk."

"You requested an urgent meeting with the president to discuss America's greatest threat. What was Mr. Bush's response?"

"He refused to meet."

"Surely he must've met with you soon thereafter?"

"No. No, he did not. And after that, all my memos sent to the president were not delivered, but rather passed down the chain of command and ultimately bounced back to me."

"So what happened?"

Clarke glanced over at Bush, took a deep breath, let it out, and smiled—apparently pleased to finally get the opportunity to tell his story in a court of law. "Some members of Mr. Bush's national security team and others agreed to meet with me. But the meeting wasn't scheduled in January or February or even March. Obviously they didn't consider it very urgent or important. Finally, in April, four months after Bush's inauguration and my request, a meeting with junior staff was convened in the Situation Room of the White House."

"Would you please tell us about it?"

"I told them that we needed to deal with the threat posed by al Qaeda. I said we needed to put pressure on both al Qaeda and the Taliban by arming the Northern Alliance and other groups in Afghanistan. Simultaneously, we needed to target bin Laden and his leadership team.

"Paul Wolfowitz, Mr. Bush's deputy secretary of defense, responded, 'I just don't understand why you're beginning to talk about this one man, bin Laden.' I replied as clearly and forcefully as I could that we were talking about a network of terrorist organizations called al Qaeda that was *led* by bin Laden—and that we were talking about that network because it and it alone posed the most immediate and serious threat to the United States. Wolfowitz said, 'There are others as well. Iraqi terrorism, for example.' I told him I was *unaware* of any Iraqi-sponsored terrorism directed at the United States since 1993, and the CIA and FBI would concur with that judgment. CIA deputy director John McLaughlin agreed with me and added, 'We have no evidence of any active Iraqi terrorism threat against the United States.'"

Shadid probed further. "US intelligence agencies were telling George Bush and his closest advisors that al Qaeda and bin Laden were a threat, and the administration would not listen?"

"That is correct. They ignored our very clear warnings."

"However, Bush's closest advisors countered by bringing up the matter of Iraq and Saddam Hussein being a threat, even though there was no evidence to suggest that he was a threat of any kind?"

"That is correct."

"Are you sure of that, Mr. Clarke?"

"In the intelligence business there is no such thing as 'sure.' But based on all the evidence we had, both empirical and actual, yes, I can state *that Saddam Hussein did not present a credible threat to the United States at that time.*"

Then Shadid asked in a slow, measured voice, "Do you have any reason to believe this information did not get to President Bush's senior advisors, and ultimately to President Bush?"

White interjected, "Objection, Your Honors. Calls for speculation."

Judge Miyako Kimura concurred, "Objection sustained."

Shadid took another tack. "Mr. Clarke, from your perspective as President Bush's chief intelligence officer, how attentive was he to incoming intel?"

"Mr. Bush had no real interest in the complicated issues and analysis related to terrorism. Early on, we were told that he was not a big reader. On issues he did care about, he believed he already had the answers. I learned over time that Mr. Bush was informed of foreign policy by talking to a small group of advisors: Dick Cheney, Don Rumsfeld, Paul Wolfowitz, Douglas Feith. He didn't like to read complex counterterrorism policy and objectives."

"Mr. Clarke, most of us are pretty familiar with the Bush team except for Douglas Feith. Can you tell us something about him?"

"He was President Bush's undersecretary of defense for policy and one of his closest advisors."

"Is it accurate to say that, given your experience, Bush ignored or dismissed the input from conventional intelligence sources and instead paid attention to the people in his inner circle, who were only giving him information he wanted to hear?"

"Yes."

"And in your opinion, was he doing this because he was seeking justification for his war?"

"Yes."

"And what were the consequences of that?"

"As a direct consequence of Mr. Bush's lack of interest in learning the truth about terrorism and terrorist groups, he ordered the invasion of Iraq, which posed no threat to the United States. It didn't have to be that way. *Nowhere on the list of things the United States should have done after September 11 was invading Iraq.* The things we should've been doing after September 11 required an enormous amount of attention and resources, but they were not available because George Bush and his people were obsessed with Iraq. As a result of Bush's war, we delivered to al Qaeda the greatest recruitment propaganda imaginable and made it difficult for other friendly Islamic governments to be seen working closely with us."

"Mr. Clarke, as you look back on Mr. Bush's refusal to deal with al Qaeda and bin Laden, and instead to pursue his obsession with Saddam Hussein, what were the results?"

"After 9/11, George Bush squandered an opportunity to eliminate al Qaeda in Afghanistan, and instead strengthened our enemies by going off on a completely unnecessary tangent—Iraq. I knew al Qaeda was growing stronger in part because of our own actions and inactions. Al Qaeda and the offspring of the Iraqi insurgency were in many ways a tougher opponent than the original threat we faced before September 11."

"As one of America's most knowledgeable and respected authorities on terrorism and counterterrorism, how do you think history will look upon George Bush's war?"

At this point, Edward White stood. "Objection, Your Honor! Asking for opinion totally irrelevant to these proceedings."

Judge Kimura sustained the objection.

Shadid rephrased the question. "Mr. Clarke, among the war crimes of which George Bush is accused are willfully causing great suffering or serious injury, extensive destruction of property not justified by military necessity, and depriving prisoners the right to a fair trial. Based on your informed observation, how did the Iraq War start, what are its consequences, and what role did George Bush play?"

Clarke seemed happy to respond. "George Bush, as president of the United States, failed to act on the very real threat from al Qaeda prior to September 11, despite repeated warnings. He harvested a political windfall after the 9/11 attacks to launch an unnecessary and costly war in Iraq that strengthened the radical anti-American Islamic terrorist movement worldwide. Before Mr. Bush invaded Iraq, America was seen as a respected superpower. As a result of his war, America is now seen as a 'superbully.' When the United States needs international support in the future, who will join us? Who will believe us? Unless America addresses these real problems, it will suffer again."

"Mr. Clarke, you participated in a CNN documentary entitled *Long Road to Hell: America in Iraq*, which first aired in the United States in October of 2015. In it, you said, 'If it were not for the American invasion of Iraq and the subsequent disbanding of the Iraqi Army by the United States, there would be no ISIS.' You couldn't be more definitive or unequivocal."

"No. No doubt about it. ISIS is a direct outgrowth of the American invasion of Iraq."

"Caused and ordered by the defendant?"

"Yes. As president of the United States and commander in chief, George Bush was responsible for causing the war to happen and then ordering it to start."

"Thank you very much, Mr. Clarke."

"Thank you for the opportunity to set the record straight."

Mission accomplished, Nadia turned confidently to the ICC judges. "No further questions, Your Honors."

"Thank you, Ms. Shadid," replied Judge Omolade Bankole. "Defense counsel, you are now free to cross-examine."

For the first time in the proceedings, defense attorney Jonathan Ortloff addressed the Court. "Thank you, Your Honor. Mr. Clarke, isn't it true you also worked for a Democratic president?"

"Yes. President Clinton."

"And isn't it true that Mr. Bush is a Republican?"

"Yes."

"And to which political party do you belong, Mr. Clarke?"

"I don't see how that's got anything to do—"

Ortloff interrupted. "You're a registered Democrat. Isn't it true that President Clinton made you the country's chief counterterrorism advisor on the National Security Council?"

"Yes."

"And that granted you cabinet-level access?"

"Yes."

"You liked having that access, didn't you, Mr. Clarke?"

Clarke did not respond. Ortloff continued, "In Washington, DC, access is power, and power is the coin of the realm. You had it, but then you lost it, didn't you, Mr. Clarke?"

"You mean when George Bush became president?"

"Yes."

"My position was redefined."

"You were demoted by President Bush, weren't you, Mr. Clarke?"

"I wouldn't say that."

"'There is no other way to say it. Your cabinet-level access was taken away from you, and, as a result, you lost much of your influence, access, and power."

"Not necessarily."

"Did you not testify earlier that you couldn't even get a memo to the president once you were working in the Bush administration?"

Prosecuting attorney McBride leapt to Mr. Clarke's defense. "Objection, Your Honor. Badgering the witness."

"Objection sustained," Judge Bankole agreed. "Mr. Ortloff, just ask your questions and refrain from editorializing."

"Yes, Your Honor." Ortloff turned quickly back to Clarke: "You were promoted by a fellow Democrat, Bill Clinton, and demoted by a Republican, George Bush? How did that make you feel, Mr. Clarke?"

"It wasn't about that. It was—"

"Isn't your appearance here today an attempt to 'get even' with a president who disregarded your experience, dismissed your professionalism, and ignored your advice?"

McBride interrupted again. "Objection, Your Honor! Defense is trying to intimidate and demean the witness."

"Objection overruled."

Undaunted, Clarke answered the question. "George Bush refused to listen to the majority of US intelligence officials who knew what was going to happen before it happened."

"Really? What was the exact date of the 9/11 attacks?"

"You've got to be kidding . . . September 11, 2001."

"And tell us, when did the 9/11 hijackers enter the United States?"

"Various times throughout 2000."

"Correct—when you were in charge of counterterrorism. They arrived on your watch and you didn't know about it, or even that they began training in flight schools in early 2001. All of that happened under your oversight, Mr. Clarke. Seems to me you couldn't have been such a great counterterrorism czar."

"Now, hold on! No one could've known about—"

Ortloff pivoted toward the judges. "Your Honors, we ask you to see this testimony for what it is. This witness is seeking to gain revenge against the defendant who demoted him—and did so for very good reasons. Mr. Clarke was incompetent and ineffective at his job."

"That's not true!" Clarke shouted. "There's no way anyone could've—"

Judge Bankole interjected forcefully, "Order! Order in the Court!"

The courtroom took thirty seconds to quiet down before Ortloff spoke. "No further questions, Your Honor."

"Thank you, Mr. Ortloff," Judge Bankole said and turned to address McBride and Shadid. "Does the prosecution wish to redirect?"

"No, Your Honor," Shadid responded, "but we would like to call the Court's attention to the rude and disrespectful questioning by defense counsel of a highly respected American intelligence official."

"Your opinion is noted, Ms. Shadid." Bankole turned to the witness. "Mr. Clarke, the Court wishes to thank you for your testimony. You are excused."

Clarke stood, glanced at Bush a final time, and marched out of the courtroom.

The final prosecution witness for the day was writer and journalist Evan Wright from Los Angeles, who had written a three-part series about the Iraq War for *Rolling Stone* magazine that was ultimately published as the book *Generation Kill*.

Ms. Shadid asked Mr. Wright to summarize a story he wrote in his book. "American Light Armored Reconnaissance units are known as LARs," he began. "Each unit has a Bushmaster 25mm rapid-fire cannon mounted in the top turret. Not only do Bushmaster cannons lay down devastating firepower . . . but the guns also have infrared radar scopes that make it easy to pick out targets a thousand meters away, even in darkness.

"One night when Iraqi soldiers attempted an assault on a road near Nasiriyah, the LAR units decimated them, killing between four hundred and five hundred Iraqis. As it was dark, many other Iraqi soldiers, unaware of the fate of their comrades, continued the attack. The fighting was fierce.

"Early the next morning, American soldiers arrived on the scene and saw dozens of dead Iraqi soldiers lying on and by the road—they had been run over repeatedly by tracked vehicles. They were flattened and almost unrecognizable as human. Nearby was a bus, smashed and burned, with charred remains still sitting upright in the seats. One Iraqi man lay dead in the road with no head. Next to him was a little girl about three or four, lying on her back. She was wearing a dress and had no legs."

Following Mr. Wright's testimony, the judges asked if the defense would like to cross-examine him. They did not.

The prosecution rested.

CHAPTER ELEVEN

Heavy Artillery

Lead me, follow me,
or get out of my way.
—General George Patton

The following morning, Judge Omolade Bankole invited the defense to call its first witness. Defense attorney Meredith Lott informed the Court their first witness would be former Army general Tommy Franks. All participants and observers were keen to hear General Franks's testimony. Questioning from defense counsel began in a rapid-fire pace.

"General Franks, thank you for making the effort to come."

"Not a problem, ma'am. 'Tommy' is fine these days."

"Okay, Tommy. You served in the United States military for thirty-eight years, correct?"

"Yes, ma'am, 1965 to 2003."

"In Vietnam, you were an artillery officer?"

"Yes, ma'am."

"And you were a senior officer in Operation Desert Storm, otherwise known as the Gulf War?"

"Yes, ma'am."

"Most of us know you were in charge of coalition forces during the Iraq War. What was your official title?"

"Commander in chief of the United States Central Command, ma'am."

"You were the boss?"

"Military boss, yes, ma'am," he said, smiling. "I had lots of other bosses above me."

"Including George W. Bush?"

"Yes, ma'am. He was the man. President of the United States."

"I'd like to start with your last meeting with President Bush before the invasion."

"Okay."

"As commander in chief of US Central Command, what did you report to the president?"

"I reported that coalition ground, naval, air, and Special Operations Forces in the region had grown rapidly and at that time totaled two hundred and ninety-two thousand. Of these, approximately one hundred and seventy thousand were US soldiers and Marines assigned to the combined forces land command."

"What was your opinion of Mr. Bush at the time?"

"Excuse me?"

"Was he calm, in control, forceful, angry?"

"I found him to be very focused. He's a guy who knows how to have a good time, but he's also very focused and very smart when he needs to be."

"Is there anything else you would like to add regarding your last meeting with Mr. Bush?"

"Yes. I told him all key infrastructure improvements had been completed and the required force was in the theater."

"You had personally spoken with the leaders of many US allies in the region?"

"Yes, ma'am. I had phone conversations with leaders in Jordan, Yemen, Pakistan, and Turkey. I had visited coalition troops in Afghanistan."

"And what was the opinion of these countries about the war? Were they, for the most part, in support of the Iraq War?"

"Yes, ma'am, for all the obvious reasons. Saddam Hussein was a cruel tyrant to his people and a destabilizing influence. His behavior was so erratic and unpredictable that he was of great concern to other countries in the region, especially with regard to oil production and sales."

"General Franks, your last prewar conversation with President Bush occurred March 19, 2003, the evening before the war started?"

"Yes, ma'am. The president was in the White House. I was on the other side of a video link at Prince Sultan Air Base in Saudi Arabia."

"What can you tell us about that meeting?"

"President Bush was with Vice President Cheney, Secretary of State Powell, and other members of his National Security Council. Once we said our hellos, the president quickly moved to the purpose of the meeting. He said, 'You've got the National Security Council here,' and asked me to give a current update of our war plans. I thought it was important to provide the commanders of each of the four US military branches a chance to speak directly with the president, so we went around the horn starting with Lieutenant General Buzz Moseley of the United States Air Force, then Lieutenant General David McKiernan of the US Army, Vice Admiral Tim Keating of the Navy, and finally Lieutenant General Earl Hailsten, commander of the Marines. President Bush asked if they were satisfied with the war plans and each responded in the affirmative."

"So, would it be accurate to say that senior command of all US military divisions—Air Force, Army, Navy, and Marines—were ready and confident to move forward with the invasion?"

"Yes, ma'am. One hundred percent ready and confident."

"And all agreed with the president's battle plan?"

"Yes, ma'am. The United States military is trained to execute war plans as directed by the commander in chief."

"Would you say that group opinion, that sense of unanimous agreement, would apply to all two hundred and ninety-two thousand troops in the region?"

"Yes, ma'am, or they wouldn't have been there."

Having gained positive ground, Lott began to deflect some of what she thought might be the prosecution's negative contentions. "Some called the invasion 'shock and awe.' Where did that come from?"

Franks shook his head. "The media called it that, ma'am. They reported that targets were hit, buildings were shaking, and explosions were bigger and louder than anyone had ever heard. Al Jazeera said, 'All Baghdad is on fire.'"

"But you were striking military targets only, correct?"

"Yes, ma'am. Per a decision made by the president and Secretary Rumsfeld, we left Iraq's electrical power grid untouched. It made sense operationally and strategically. The president stated, 'We're not going to destroy Iraq. We're going to liberate the country from Saddam Hussein's regime.' So in building our targets, we excluded power plants, transformer stations, and electrical pylons and lines. The plan to preserve Iraq's infrastructure outweighed any possible military tactical disadvantage."

"Most of us have our own opinion of the war. What is yours?"

Michael McBride interrupted. "Objection, Your Honors. Calls for personal opinion and speculation."

"Objection overruled," Judge Bankole said. "The witness can answer the question."

Franks nodded at the judge and looked over at George Bush before continuing. "Thanks to the decisions America's leaders made, the people of Afghanistan and Iraq are free today. And rogue states around the world have been served notice. We need not apologize for the successes.

"History will record that America's strategy for fighting terrorism was a good one, and that the execution of Operation Iraqi Freedom by our young men and women in uniform was unequaled in its excellence by anything in the annals of war. People on the hometown streets of America know the truth. Today, Saddam Hussein is gone. Coalition forces rebuilt or constructed thousands of schools and hospitals. Today, thanks largely to the coalition, Iraqi medical professionals and healthcare far surpass what was available during Saddam's reign."

Obviously pleased with the former general's testimony thus far, Lott probed for more. "General Franks, it needs to be asked—one of President Bush's reasons for going to war was the threat of their possession of and use of weapons of mass destruction. What were and are your thoughts about WMD?"

"I am frequently asked what I found to be most surprising during my tenure as commander in chief of the US military in Iraq. Each time, I answer the absence of WMD. We went to war with reasonable expectations that we would find those weapons. Now some say we were duped into believing they existed and that we were wrong to have toppled Saddam Hussein's regime and free Iraq. I do not agree. As we all know, David Kay was the weapons inspector who led the US-Iraq survey group. He told a Senate committee his view was that based on the best evidence he had,

Iraq did indeed have weapons of mass destruction. They were elaborately shielded by deceptive operations that continued during and even after the Iraq War."

"But there was no question you needed to take out Saddam Hussein."

"No, ma'am. There was plenty of evidence that Saddam and his sons had slaughtered a minimum of two hundred and ninety thousand innocent Iraqi men, women, and children. I'm proud of the fact that a dictator who had used WMD to murder his own people will never have a chance to use them on Americans. Tens of thousands of average Americans I met after the war have convinced me that the majority of my fellow citizens understand the principles of that war and agree we did the right thing. I recall an eighteenth-century British philosopher, Edmund Burke, who reminds us that 'the only thing necessary for the triumph of evil is for good men to do nothing.'"

Lott allowed Franks's powerful testimony to pervade the room before continuing. "General Franks, by any standard you are a good man, a great American. Is there anything else you would like to say?"

"Yes, ma'am. We were blessed in America with great leadership that evidenced character and moral courage and a depth of resolve seldom seen. We see evidence today of a core value that in my opinion was dormant after 9/11 and before the Iraq War—*patriotism*, constant patriotism by those who now salute the flag and wave it proudly." Franks then dramatically pointed his finger at the defendant. "And that leadership was provided in large part by the very man who sits before you in this courtroom, former president of the United States, George W. Bush. And I want to take this occasion to personally thank him for it."

That said, General Franks stood and offered a snappy salute to his commander in chief, who smiled and returned the gesture in kind.

Meredith Lott added an exclamation point. "Thank *you*, sir."

"Pleasure, ma'am."

"No further questions, Your Honors."

"Thank you, Ms. Lott," Judge Bankole responded, and then addressed the opposing attorneys. "Does the prosecution wish to cross-examine this witness?"

"Yes, Your Honor," McBride said. "We would."

"Please proceed."

"Thank you, Your Honor." McBride offered a faint smile to the witness. "Mr. Franks, the prosecution would also like to thank you for coming."

"Okay, sir."

"Please know we have only one goal here and it is to determine, to the greatest degree possible, the truth of what happened before and during the Iraq War."

"Yes, sir. The truth will set us free."

"Thank you, sir. Now, Mr. Franks, I don't want to be disrespectful in any way, but I do want to determine what happened. You say, 'May God bless America.' As a spiritual man, do you wish for God to bless all the peoples of the world?"

"Of course."

"Jesus preached that we should love all people."

"Yes, sir."

"Would that include people in Great Britain and Europe?"

"Of course."

"People in the Middle East? After all, Jesus was born and lived in the Middle East."

"Yes."

"Do you wish for God to bestow his love on the peoples of Iraq?"

"Yes, of course."

"Thank you; so do I. Your first meeting with George Bush occurred December 28, 2001, at his ranch in Crawford, Texas?"

"Yes, sir."

"Toward the end of that meeting you referred to a chart labeled 'overreaching concept.' Do you remember what it said?"

"Yes, sir. 'Regime change' and 'WMD removal' were the working targets."

"And all in attendance agreed with those goals?"

"Yes, sir."

"Did it ever occur to you, or the group, that as Osama bin Laden and al Qaeda were responsible for the 9/11 attacks, logically they should have been the targets to find and bring to justice?"

"Yes, sir, but I was not president of the United States."

"So even though George Bush knew bin Laden was hiding in the mountains of Afghanistan or Pakistan, he basically ignored him and turned his attention, and yours, to Saddam Hussein and Iraq."

"No, sir. Incorrect. President Bush was interested in bin Laden as well."

"But when you couldn't get bin Laden, in time Bush turned his attention more and more to Saddam Hussein and Iraq."

"Yes, in time."

"So in March 2003, you led coalition forces totaling two hundred and ninety-two thousand soldiers to remove Saddam and find and destroy his WMD?"

"Basically, yes."

"Basically, factually, and actually—yes. Putting aside Saddam and WMD for the moment, if your sole target had been to capture or kill Osama bin Laden, given all the assets you had available, what would that have taken?"

"That's a hypothetical question."

"I beg to differ, sir. It's a straightforward question—what in terms of manpower and time would it have taken to get bin Laden?"

Franks studied McBride for a long moment, trying to decide if he should answer the question or not. Finally, he said, "Well—couple months' planning, I guess, consistently good intel, a few dozen SEALs, and some luck."

"And the thirst the American people had for revenge after the 9/11 attacks would have been satisfied?"

"That is your theory, sir."

"Yes. A theory shared by most thinking people."

"Objection, Your Honors," Edward White interjected. "Conjecture."

Judge Hurst-Brown sustained the objection.

McBride quickly moved on. "Moving back to WMD. While nobody is saying Saddam didn't have and use WMD in the 1980s and '90s, there was a huge question of whether he actually had WMD at the beginning of the twenty-first century."

"Yes, sir, that was a question."

"And yet no one had found evidence that Saddam had WMD. UN inspectors who had been given free rein in Iraq had certainly not found WMD. Can we agree that no hard, confirmed intelligence proved beyond any doubt that Saddam had WMD?"

"Yes."

"Mr. Franks, for the record and with the eyes of all human-kind on you, and your God watching over you, did you find even one weapon of mass destruction in Iraq?"

"Well, sir, I was surprised that WMD were not used against our troops. And I was surprised that we did not find stockpiles of such weapons in Iraq."

"We'll take that as a 'no.' So, after all was said and done, no weapons of mass destruction were found?"

"That's correct."

"Mr. Franks, you may know that the senior Pentagon correspondent for the *Washington Post*, Thomas E. Ricks, wrote a very fine book about the Iraq War entitled *Fiasco*. In it, he refers to a period of time during the buildup to the war in 2002 when the Bush administration's view departed from that of the US intelligence community at large. Mr. Ricks cited a senior Pentagon analyst who said, 'There wasn't anyone in the intelligence community who was saying to Mr. Bush what Pentagon analyst Douglas Feith was saying to Mr. Bush.' And quoting Marine general Gregory Newbold, the Joint Staff's operations director, 'It was also my sense that they'—referring to the Bush administration—'*cherry-picked obscure, unconfirmed information to reinforce their own philosophies.*'

"So it is clear that Bush had people like Douglas Feith at the Pentagon, and others in his administration, serving up intel to him that they knew he wanted to hear."

Franks reluctantly nodded. "They were giving the president intel, that's correct."

"And isn't it true that much of it *did not* reflect what the great majority of US intelligence agencies believed and said at the time?"

"I'm aware that there were contradictory views."

"Isn't it true, Mr. Franks, that you referred to Douglas Feith as 'the dumbest fucking guy on the planet'? Did you say that, sir?"

"Yes."

"One of Douglas Feith's colleagues, retired Army lieutenant Jay Garner, also said, 'I think he's incredibly dangerous. He's a very smart guy whose electrons aren't connected.'"

"No comment."

"So the opinions of senior military officials—including yourself—were that one of Bush's most relied-upon sources of information was considered to be 'the dumbest fucking guy on the planet whose electrons weren't connected' and who was 'incredibly dangerous' by people who should know?"

Franks and McBride glared at each other until the prosecutor continued. "Mr. Franks, you probably know only too well that the official count of US soldiers killed in Iraq is said to be forty-five hundred. In addition, tens of thousands of American soldiers were wounded, physically and/or mentally. Many of them are still suffering today."

"Yes."

"Do you know how many Iraqi soldiers were killed in that war?"

"I believe around twenty thousand."

"Yes. And the number of Iraqi civilians killed?"

"I'm not sure."

"That's to be expected because it's a difficult number to determine. It is estimated to be more than half a million. Putting aside the cost in human lives, the war cost the United States more than four trillion dollars. Deep down in your heart of hearts, Tommy Franks, was that war necessary?"

Ed White stood. "Objection, Your Honor. Calls for personal speculation."

Judge Bankole agreed. "Objection sustained."

McBride quickly continued. "Mr. Franks, do you believe military commanders should exercise their own personal judgment of right and wrong when given orders by their superiors?"

"It depends."

"On what?"

"A wide range of variables."

"If your commander in chief asked you to cut the heads off all the enemy and rape all the women, would you do that, sir?"

"That's another hypothetical and ridiculous question."

"Hypothetical, yes. But it's about as ridiculous as George Bush sending you to fight a war with massive military strength to do something that *did not need* to be done. That war had nothing to do with Saddam being a threat, or WMD, and he knew it."

"That may be your view, but it's not mine, and not the view of most Americans I know."

"Then you don't know many Americans. More than 60 percent opposed that war."

McBride pivoted to another subject. "How familiar are you with the prisoner abuses at the Abu Ghraib prison facility?"

"It was a shameful chapter in the history of the United States."

"Care to elaborate?"

"Those outrages can never be excused. Millions of men and women have worn the uniforms of America's military with honor and compassion. As has been said so often, it only takes a few to smear the reputation of all—unfortunate, but true."

"Mr. Franks, I realize a great military leader such as yourself must remain steadfastly loyal to your commanding officers, certainly including the president of the United States. But I ask you, as you look back on the Iraq War, what are your personal thoughts?"

Franks looked over at Bush, wondering how much to say—how far to go. Bush sat motionless, staring back, presumably wondering himself. Franks answered in a quiet, measured voice,

"I did not agree with every decision made before and during that war. Many say President Bush should be blamed. I do not. I'm constantly amazed at the shallow thinking that underpins that opinion. Things go wrong in war. If war were easy and convenient, there would be too many of them."

McBride pushed for more. "No regrets?"

"Sure. I wish some things had been done differently. I wish the international community had infused more money more quickly into Iraq, and that Iraq's military hadn't melted away as our troops moved on Baghdad. I wish these young Iraqi men had committed themselves to building a new Iraq."

McBride said nothing, sensing Franks might want or need to say more. Sure enough, after a long, awkward pause, he cleared his throat and continued. "In the difficult days after the war some asked me to lay blame—to point to guilty parties or condemn perceived misdeeds. I have said, and will continue to say, there's enough blame to go around. We live in a democratic society, a free country. We elect our leaders for their proven judgment, and we expect them to use that judgment for the common good."

"Thank you, Mr. Franks. On a personal note, I hope you do not personally bear any shame or regret over that war. You only did what you were ordered to do by your commander in chief." McBride turned to the bench. "No further questions, Your Honors. Prosecution rests."

"Thank you, Mr. McBride," Judge Bankole said. "Does the defense wish to redirect?"

"Yes, Your Honor," White answered. "Just one thing more. General Franks, did you believe you were in command of this war, or did you feel you had to get approval from the White House for your operations?"

"You mean like General Westmoreland going back to President Johnson every week during the Vietnam War asking for permission to do this or that? No. President Bush made it clear he trusted his commanders to do the right thing and that they would not be second-guessed by him."

"So you felt you were totally in control of this war?"

"Yes, sir."

"Thank you, General Franks. Nothing further."

"Thank you, Mr. White," Judge Bankole replied and turned again to the prosecutors. "Does the prosecution wish to re-cross-examine this witness?"

"Yes, Your Honor," McBride answered.

"Please proceed."

"Mr. Franks, on your reading of the US Constitution, who is ultimately in charge of the armed forces?"

"Well, that would be the president."

"That's why they also refer to him as the commander in chief. He is literally at the top of the command chain, correct?"

"That's right."

"And George Bush knew what was happening in Iraq through his daily and sometimes even hourly briefings from you, the Defense Department, and the intelligence community?"

"As we covered before, yes."

"So he could've stopped all military operations at any time?"

"Yes."

"Mr. Franks, I would appreciate an answer to this question, which has been bothering me for a long time. The Iraq War started in March 2003. In one month's time Baghdad fell and Saddam's statue was toppled to the ground. Nine months into the war, Saddam was captured. For all intents and purposes, wasn't the war over by then? After your forces brought Iraq to its knees in a matter of months, *the war continued for eight more years.* Why didn't America just go over there and do what it thought it had to do, and get the hell out?"

"You'll have to ask someone other than me. Higher powers."

"Thank you, Mr. Franks." McBride turned to the judges. "Nothing further, Your Honors."

"Does the defense wish to redirect this witness?" Judge Hurst-Brown asked.

"No, Your Honor," White responded. "Defense wishes to thank General Tommy Franks for his testimony and call its next witness."

"The Court thanks Mr. Franks for his testimony as well and wishes him a safe journey home. Defense may proceed with its next witness."

Edward White replied, "Thank you, Your Honor. Defense calls Dr. Condoleezza Rice to the witness bench."

CHAPTER TWELVE

Quid Pro Quo

Be with a leader when he is right,
stay with him when he is still right,
but leave him when he is wrong.
—Abraham Lincoln

Looking for ways to expand coverage and feed the insatiable public hunger for all things Bush-case related, news organizations began to take polls to determine public opinion regarding the status of the case. Nowhere was this more apparent than in the United States.

When taken as a whole, the results of polls across all fifty states mirrored what usually occurs in presidential elections. Not surprisingly, states that customarily vote Republican, such as Alabama, Utah, and Oklahoma, polled in favor of Mr. Bush's innocence. States that customarily vote Democratic, such as New York, Illinois, and California, favored a guilty verdict.

Those swing states in which voting would depend on the candidate or subject matter, such as Florida, Ohio, and Colorado, were divided in their opinion. Allowing for customary statistical variants, it could be said that at this juncture the American public considered the Bush case to be a neck-and-neck race. That is, until the defense called its next witness to the stand.

Condoleezza Rice was born in Birmingham, Alabama, in 1954, the only child of a mother who was a high school science, music, and speech teacher and a father who was a football and basketball coach as well as a Presbyterian minister. Dr. Rice, who never married and had no children, was America's first female national security advisor and first female African American secretary of state. Her name, "Condoleezza," comes from a musical term, *con doleezza*, Italian for "with sweetness." She served George W. Bush as chief foreign policy advisor in his 2000 campaign for the presidency and left a prestigious appointment at Stanford University to join his administration when he was elected. Dr. Rice was a close confidant of George Bush during his entire eight years as president. Some say his closest.

Dr. Rice, dressed in a natty suit and exuding supreme confidence, read the swearing-in document and took her seat on the witness bench. Lead defense attorney Ed White began. "Greetings and thank you for coming."

"I regard it as my duty to be here."

"Please help me with proper protocol—shall I refer to you as Madam Secretary, Dr. Rice, Ms. Rice, or Condoleezza?"

"Condoleezza is fine."

"Thank you. Condoleezza. You served under George W. Bush during his entire presidency. In his first term, 2001 to 2005, you were his national security advisor, and in his second term, 2005 to 2009, you were his secretary of state, correct?"

"Yes."

"Would it be accurate to say, during the span of his eight years in office, no one was in such close communication with the president as yourself?"

"Yes."

"And you are fully aware of what this proceeding is about?"

"Yes, I am."

"As we speak here today, years after the Iraq War, would you please put into context the challenges President Bush faced as they related to Saddam Hussein and Iraq?"

Dr. Rice glanced over at her dear friend and former boss sitting at the accused table, and launched into her testimony like a professor lecturing graduate law students at Stanford. "It is easy to forget now with all the attendant controversy surrounding the Iraq War, but concerns had been growing for a decade, that were shared by the international community and both sides of the aisle in the United States Congress, that Saddam Hussein's Iraq was again emerging as a major threat to the Middle East. The air strike on Iraq that President Clinton ordered in December 1998 garnered a House vote of four hundred seventeen to five resolving that the United States should support efforts to remove Saddam and promote the emergence of a democratic government."

Impressed with his star witness, Ed White framed his next question. "So any president charged with protecting and defending the best interests of the American people would have had grave concerns about Saddam Hussein, especially when considering his propensity to build and use the most destructive weaponry known to man?"

"Exactly. After the 9/11 attacks, President Bush made it clear that the immediate problem was the al Qaeda sanctuary in Afghanistan. But in the spring of 2002, upon examining Iraq's WMD threat and its nexus with terrorism, the question of what to do about Saddam—who had a record of using chemical weapons against Iranian targets and ethnic minorities within his own population—was on the table again."

"And this concern was supported by intelligence officials reporting to the president?"

"Essentially, yes. The process of providing intelligence estimates is an imprecise science at best. At the time of the Iraq War,
the United States had twelve intelligence agencies that tried to
produce a joint assessment known as the National Intelligence
Estimate—usually referred to as the NIE. Understandably there
are almost always differences of opinion among these agencies.
President Bush, from the time he took office, had received almost
daily, increasingly alarming reports about Saddam's progress
in reconstituting his WMD program. In October 2002, the
NIE informed us that Iraq had continued its weapons of mass
destruction programs in defiance of UN resolutions. Saddam
had chemical and biological weapons as well as missiles with
ranges in excess of UN restrictions. If left unchecked, Iraq probably would have a nuclear weapon within a few years."

White seized an opening provided by Dr. Rice. "Yes, thank
you for bringing up the NIE. While the prosecution has presented its slanted evidence of US intelligence, defense wishes to
introduce the NIE report as Defense Evidence #1." Meredith
Lott delivered the document to the Court as White continued. "Condoleezza, I would like to read one of many sections
from the NIE that forecasted great danger: 'We judge that all
key aspects—R&D, production, and weaponization—of Iraq's
offensive biological weapons program are active and that most
elements are larger and more advanced than they were before
the Gulf War.'"

"Yes," Dr. Rice commented and quickly continued. "It also
stated that Baghdad had mobile facilities for producing bacterial
and toxic biological warfare agents."

"We must all keep in mind that during the aftermath of 9/11,
America and all peaceful nations were consumed with the new
threat of terrorists and terrorism."

"Correct. Saddam was a known supporter of terrorism. He paid families of Palestine suicide bombers twenty-five thousand dollars apiece after every successful attack. He had harbored numerous known terrorists over the years. In the shadow of 9/11, the possibility that Saddam might arm terrorists with chemical or biological weapons, or even a nuclear device, and set them loose against the United States was very real to us. We failed to connect the dots before the 9/11 attacks and had never imagined the use of civilian airliners as missiles against the World Trade Center and the Pentagon. The thought that an unconstrained Saddam Hussein might aid terrorists in an attack on the United States did not seem far-fetched to us."

White was visibly pleased. Needing to counter the effect of the prosecution's witness testimony, and to build preemptive momentum for the defense, White pressed down harder on the accelerator. "And given Saddam's history, it was highly unlikely he would succumb to any threat posed by the United States or other countries. Nonetheless, the Bush administration sought to use international pressure before resorting to war?"

"Yes. No one believed that Saddam would give up power peacefully. We were down to two options if we wanted to change course: increase international pressure to make him give up his WMD or overthrow him by force."

"And what was President Bush's view of all this?"

"The question of how to remove Saddam short of war was constantly on his mind. We reached out to Arab leaders asking them to assure Saddam that the United States would indeed overthrow him if he didn't comply with UN-mandated sanctions. The Egyptians claimed that Saddam's son had sent a message that he would leave Iraq in exchange for one billion dollars. President Bush sent word that he would gladly pay. Nothing came of it."

"And given Saddam's well-known disdain and disregard for international pressure, America was confronted with the possibility of having to use force?"

"At the beginning of 2003, I was convinced we would have to use military force. Saddam seemed to be playing games with the UN and US inspectors . . . refusing interviews with his scientists, sending 'minders' along with them for meetings with inspectors. That is what passed for cooperation, and it seemed to be producing minimal information. Nonetheless, the inspectors, despite limitations, gathered evidence that Iraqi officials were moving various items and hiding them at suspect sites prior to inspection visits. The Iraqi dictator seemed to be up to his old tricks. Frankly I couldn't understand it. Maybe he just didn't believe us."

"So it would be your opinion that Saddam Hussein posed the greatest threat to world peace at the time in question?"

"Yes. Saddam Hussein was a cancer in the Middle East who had attacked his neighbors and thrown the region into chaos. He had drawn the United States into conflict twice, once to expel him from Kuwait and a second time to deliver air strikes against suspected WMD sites. Saddam routinely shot at our aircraft patrolling under UN authority. The UN sanctions put into place to contain him had crumbled under the weight of international corruption and his considerable guile. He had tried to assassinate a former president of the United States, and he supported terrorists—harboring some of the most notorious in his country. There had been no arms inspection in Iraq for more than four years. All but one US intelligence agency believed he had reconstituted his nuclear weapons capability and could possibly have a crude nuclear device within a year. Similar views were shared by many foreign intelligence organizations. The world had given Saddam one last chance to come clean about his weapons program or face serious consequences. This time, the word of the international community had to mean something."

"Obviously, President Bush believed he had ample justification for this war from the perspectives of both national and international law."

"Yes, and it was a logical assumption. The United States had long maintained the option of preemptive action to counter threats to its national security. And international law has for centuries recognized that nations *need not suffer an attack* before they took action against an imminent threat. In an age when enemies of civilized countries openly and actively seek to use the world's most destructive technologies, the United States could not remain idle while danger gathered. These enemies were of a different character than in the past—when threats had come largely from states in which there was some reasonable expectation that military preparation for an attack would be visible. Terrorists today operate in the shadows and can attack without warning, as they had on September 11. In light of this threat, limiting preemption only to those occasions when we were *sure* an enemy was about to attack made little sense."

"From your front-row seat during all of this activity, as national security advisor and then secretary of state, were you 100 percent behind President Bush's decision to wage war against Iraq?"

"Yes, 100 percent behind the president."

Dr. Rice's authoritative, confident, and hugely intelligent testimony went a long way to validate her friend George Bush, and invalidate what some thought to be a nonsensical trial. Ed White, looking like a proud father after his daughter graduated summa cum laude, warmly acknowledged his prized witness.

"Thank you, Dr. Rice." He then turned toward the judges and confidently concluded, "No further questions, Your Honors."

"Thank you, Mr. White," Judge Hurst-Brown said. "Does the prosecution wish to cross-examine?"

"Yes, Your Honor, we do," Ms. Shadid responded.

"Please proceed."

There had been a debate between Michael and Nadia regarding which of the two should take the testimony of Dr. Rice. For starters, both wanted to accept the maximum amount of personal responsibility in any contest to ensure victory over defeat. In the end they concluded that Nadia, as an Iraqi and a woman, should have the honor and immense challenge of questioning the former secretary of state.

Nadia Shadid did not start with any sort of welcoming smile, as she knew Dr. Rice would only see that as patronizing, but rather simply said, "Dr. Rice, the prosecution also wishes to thank you for coming to testify at this tribunal. For those who may not know, and as inconceivable as it may seem, the ICC cannot itself subpoena or otherwise force a witness to testify. Witnesses appear at their own free will. So again, we thank you."

Rice snapped back, "As stated earlier, I think it is my duty to testify on behalf of former president Bush. But my appearance here today in no way endorses what the ICC is doing, nor should it be understood to legitimize these proceedings in any way."

Shadid ignored the condescending rebuke and went to work. "Dr. Rice, would you agree that the 9/11 attacks were masterminded and executed by al Qaeda, whose leader was Osama bin Laden—without any involvement of Saddam Hussein?"

"There was debate over the question of whether Saddam had a hand in the September 11 attacks. Some suggested that Saddam and al Qaeda were likely allies. I was never convinced by that argument."

"Thank you. America is a proud and powerful country. It is rightfully considered the leader of the free world. Would you agree that America had all the justification necessary to hunt down and destroy al Qaeda after the crimes they committed on 9/11?"

"Yes."

"Do you realize that in the entirety of your testimony for the defense, al Qaeda was mentioned only once, and Osama bin Laden was *never* mentioned?"

"No, but . . . okay."

"Changing the focus from al Qaeda and bin Laden to Saddam and Iraq is a switch of monumental proportions. Can you help us understand when, how, and why George Bush did that?"

Rice paused for a moment, knowing the question could be a trap, and then spoke. "The 9/11 attacks began at 8:46 a.m. eastern time. The first statement from President Bush came at 1:04 p.m. After asking for prayers for those killed or wounded, he stated that the United States would hunt down and punish those responsible for the cowardly acts. On the morning of September 12, the president held an intelligence briefing, which for the first time included the FBI director and the attorney general. Having not anticipated the attacks of 9/11, the intelligence agencies were determined not to be wrong again. CIA director George Tenet briefed us on the evidence of al Qaeda's complicity in the attacks. The president listened to the case against al Qaeda and informed the War Council that we had crossed the threshold and would destroy the terrorists. The president's instructions were clear: Prepare to go to war against al Qaeda in a meaningful way, including the destruction of its safe haven in Afghanistan."

"And what about bin Laden?"

"When his Saudi Arabian citizenship was revoked, bin Laden returned to Afghanistan, where he built a base of operations for his terrorist network. Sharing some ideological kinship with bin Laden, the Taliban condoned and even supported his efforts to establish al Qaeda training camps in Afghanistan. The immediate problem we faced after 9/11 was to defeat the Taliban and ultimately destroy al Qaeda."

"How and when did the focus shift from al Qaeda to Iraq and Saddam?"

"In a meeting on September 12, after some debate about how to proceed, Secretary of Defense Rumsfeld turned the floor over to his deputy, Paul Wolfowitz, who started talking about Iraq and focusing on the relative strategic importance of Iraq over Afghanistan. He suggested that a war in Afghanistan would be much more complicated than a 'straightforward' engagement against a real army such as Saddam's in Iraq. It was awkward because everyone had come to the meeting thinking that the war would be fought in Afghanistan. Honestly, I remember thinking Wolfowitz's comment was a huge distraction when there was so much to be done."

"Then what?"

"The president asked each member of his War Council for recommendations. Colin Powell suggested that the Taliban be given an ultimatum. He also stated that he was fundamentally opposed to action in Iraq. The president turned to Vice President Cheney, who affirmed the war option and the need for an ultimatum. The president ended the meeting by confirming that this time al Qaeda must be defeated."

"So your recollection is that Deputy Secretary of Defense Wolfowitz first mentioned the need to focus on Saddam and Iraq, thus shifting the discussion away from al Qaeda and bin Laden?"

Rice, not wanting to be pandered to, snapped back, "Yes, as I said."

"What happened next?" Shadid asked.

"The president asked for and Congress passed a resolution authorizing the use of military force on September 14, three days after the 9/11 attacks. This unified the country and the government's resolve to go after al Qaeda. On October 7, the president went before the American public to announce 'Operation Enduring Freedom.' The United States was going to invade Afghanistan because the Taliban had refused to meet our demands to surrender al Qaeda's leaders and close terrorist training camps. It was President Bush's decision not to fight a big ground war but to rely instead on Afghan fighters, US Special Forces, intelligence, and air power."

"And the results of that strategy?"

"The initial phases of the plan were frustrating. US planes bombed the few installations that could be hit from the air. However, because Afghanistan's terrain was so rugged, mountainous, rural, and underdeveloped, the military quickly ran out of targets. When it was time to begin the ground assault, our 'cavalry' wasn't moving—saying they needed more equipment and better intelligence. George Tenet asked, 'Why don't they have the intelligence they need?' The answer was that the intelligence would come as they began to move forward and engage the Taliban forces. Growing impatient, the president complained, 'They just need to *move*.' The absence of action on the ground for days led to news coverage that trumpeted the 'quagmire' into which US forces had fallen."

"So to be clear: President Bush *did not* wage a full-scale invasion in Afghanistan to find and destroy the perpetrators of the 9/11 attacks, but instead relied on 'Afghan fighters, US Special Forces, intelligence, and air power'?"

"That's what I said."

"One would think the president would use the full force of the US military to bring justice to those who committed the crimes of 9/11."

"The president obviously thought his was the best strategy, and he was the commander in chief."

"And when his strategy stalled—when he was not successful in either destroying al Qaeda or killing bin Laden, George Bush started to focus on Iraq and Saddam, correct?"

"Eventually, he turned his attention to Iraq."

Seizing the opportunity to attack, Shadid posed the following question in a slow, clear, and definitive voice, "The logical question then is—why Saddam? When he had absolutely nothing to do with the 9/11 attacks and hadn't been an enemy of the United States for more than a decade—why Saddam?"

Rice responded quickly and confidently, "It was well understood at the time that Iraq was systematically violating the ceasefire agreement that it had signed in 1991 and evading UN sanctions that had been levied against it. Periodic crises had flared up in intervening years, leading arms inspectors to leave Iraq in 1998, allowing Saddam's WMD program to be unmonitored. When President Bush took office in January 2001, that was the situation we inherited and tried to address by strengthening the containment of Saddam's regime."

"And were those efforts successful?"

"Those efforts were frustrating and largely unsuccessful."

"Thank you for your candor, Dr. Rice. During your testimony to the defense, you referred to President Clinton's bombing of Iraq in 1998. That was three years before the 9/11 attacks, and five years before the US invasion of Iraq in 2003. It's all too clear that much can happen in one year, much less the passing of five years! What exactly was Saddam Hussein doing in 2002 and leading up to the day of the invasion in March of 2003 to make him and Iraq a 'clear and present danger' to the United States?"

Dr. Rice paused to consider her response and then proceeded. "Iraq was on President Bush's mind. He was wondering how to use the threat of force to compel Saddam to comply with his obligations and destroy his suspected WMD."

Knowing she had Rice on the ropes, Shadid turned up the heat. "You used the word 'suspected' because *no one knew for certain* that Saddam had WMD."

"Intelligence analysis of such covert activities is *the art, not the science* of piecing together information and drawing a picture of what is transpiring."

This was a crucial moment in Dr. Rice's testimony, as she herself had introduced the concept that intelligence gathering and reporting were often not as much about the facts as about speculation—the inference being, how could her former boss George Bush take his country to war on intelligence that was considered to be *more speculative than factual?*

Shadid seized the opening and attacked with renewed vigor. "Okay, Dr. Rice, let's talk about that. You mentioned in your testimony that at the time in question the United States had many separate intelligence agencies providing estimates of Iraq's capabilities, and that those agencies often disagreed in their assessments."

"Yes."

"Isn't it true that the National Intelligence Estimate that was mentioned, known as the NIE, included the findings of both the Bureau of Intelligence and Research and the intelligence arm of the US State Department?"

"Yes."

"And isn't it true that this bureau, known as the 'INR,' had more than three hundred employees and a sixty-million-dollar annual budget?"

"Yes."

Shadid turned to the ICC judges to introduce additional prosecutorial evidence as McBride handed a new document to the clerk. "Your Honors, the prosecution wishes to submit Prosecution Evidence #4, the entire US State Department's INR report regarding its assessment of Saddam Hussein and Iraq at the time in question. With the permission of the Court, we wish to read a portion of the report into the record."

Hurst-Brown put his hand over the microphone in front of him, conferred in hushed tones with the other judges, and then announced, "Permission granted."

"Thank you, Your Honor. Quoting from the State Department's INR report: 'The activities we detected do not add up to a compelling case that Iraq is currently pursuing an integrated and comprehensive approach to acquire nuclear weapons. Lacking persuasive evidence that Baghdad has launched a coherent effort to reconstitute its nuclear weapons program, the INR is *unwilling to speculate* that such an effort began soon after the departure of UN inspectors, or to project a timeline for the completion of these activities.'"

Shadid turned back to Rice. "Dr. Rice, can you confirm that President Bush was given this intelligence report?"

"All available intelligence information was given to the president."

"And thus we assume he got it and looked at it?"

"I assume nothing."

"Dr. Rice, true or false . . . US intelligence agencies were inconsistent and conflicted with regard to Iraq's possession of WMD."

Rice stared at Shadid for an awkward moment before stating in a measured voice, "This is a matter of public record. There were inconsistencies in the intelligence reporting and no one could be sure what Saddam had."

With that concession from Dr. Rice, an eerie hush fell over the Court, as it was clear to all what a defining moment it was in the case. As Nadia Shadid had been a teenager when Bush waged his war on her country, she had waited a long time to get a high-ranking US government official on the record regarding this subject.

She paused long enough to let the significance of the moment register with the judges and then transitioned to a new line of questioning, "Thank you, Dr. Rice. Both you and defense counsel speak of 'imminent threat' when attempting to justify the Iraq War. Incontrovertible evidence proves that Saddam Hussein posed *no threat* to the United States in March of 2003. The Iraq War started in March of 2003 and lasted until December of 2011, eight years and nine months. It was a war that devastated the country and created a lawless territory into which revolutionaries and terrorists coalesced to create a rogue military force, which became known as the Islamic State. We are all aware of the devastation the Islamic State has caused and continues to cause.

"Dr. Rice, the prosecution in this case has proven beyond any doubt that the defendant, George Bush, as president of the United States and commander in chief, is *the person* most responsible for causing this war. Under oath and for the millions of people who are now hearing, or will hear, your testimony, please tell us why this war happened."

The two women glared at each other while Rice considered her answer. "UN-mandated sanctions were not working, the weapons inspections were unsatisfactory, and we could not get Saddam to leave by any other means."

"Dr. Rice, you are one of the most knowledgeable experts in the world on international law, and thus know that those reasons are not legal justifications for war. Again, was there any legitimate reason for that war?"

"We were trying to preempt Saddam and Iraq from any aggression against the United States and/or her allies and felt a sense of urgency driven by the fact that our military forces were approaching levels of mobilization that could not be sustained much longer. A decision had to be made to either keep moving forward with the mobilization in Afghanistan or start pulling back. It wasn't possible to just stand still, since doing so would leave our forces vulnerable in theater without sufficient logistical support. The fact is, we invaded Iraq because we believed we had run out of other options. We did not go to Iraq to bring democracy any more than Roosevelt went to war against Hitler to democratize Germany. We went to war because we saw Saddam Hussein as a threat to our national security and that of our allies. The president did not want to go to war. We had come to the conclusion that it was time to deal with Saddam and believed that the world would be better off with the dictator out of power."

"Again, Dr. Rice, you know none of that is legal justification for war."

"Please do not be condescending to me, Ms. Shadid."

Ignoring Rice's rebuke, Shadid pressed on with her agenda. "Clearly George Bush was getting conflicting information and advice from his vice president, secretaries, intelligence sources, and military advisors. But isn't it true, Dr. Rice, that the president paid the most attention to his own counsel?"

"He listens to lots of people and even prays over hard decisions. But in the end he comes to his own decision and sticks to it no matter what."

"Yes, exactly. His was the final decision. He was 'the decider.' That's why he is sitting here before the ICC today."

Sensing the time was right, Shadid went in for the kill. "Dr. Rice, no doubt you are aware of the litany of war crimes that were committed as a direct result of George Bush's decisions and orders. In finality, the judgment of this tribunal will not be based on Bush's *causing* the war to happen, but whether or not the crimes committed resulting from his war are illegal and thus criminal. Dr. Rice, we thank you for your testimony and your honesty."

With apparent satisfaction for a job well done and a sense of relief that this was over, Shadid turned toward the bench and simply stated, "No further questions, Your Honors."

"Thank you, Ms. Shadid," Judge Hurst-Brown said. "Does defense counsel wish to redirect questions to this witness?"

"No, sir, we do not," White responded.

"And does the defense wish to call any other witnesses?"

"No, Your Honor, we do not."

Hurst-Brown rapped his gavel. "*The Prosecutor v. George W. Bush* is adjourned until further notice."

CHAPTER THIRTEEN

Family Matters

*Whenever men take the law into their own hands, the loser
is the law. And when the law loses, freedom languishes.*
—Robert F. Kennedy

America has certainly had its share of contentious times during its relatively young life: the Civil War in the 1860s, the McCarthy hearings in the 1950s, the Vietnam War in the 1960s and '70s, male chauvinists versus women's libbers, gays versus straights, and the list goes on. But one of the defining characteristics of America is that she permits dissent. Perhaps more than in any other country in the world, citizens in America are free to express their opinions and advocate for what they believe. America's founding fathers fought and died for this right, and it has been a defining characteristic of America's DNA from the beginning.

This fundamental right was put to the test yet again when a former president of the United States was brought before an international tribunal to stand trial for crimes he may or may not have committed. The story of the Bush trial consumed the public's attention on a level seldom if ever seen in the country's history. One could literally not watch, hear, or read media in any form at any time of the day or night without being bombarded with news of the trial. During working hours, people went online, listened to radios, checked mobile devices, snuck a peek at TV, and discussed and debated developments with anyone willing.

The huge monitor in New York City's Times Square provided nonstop real-time coverage.

The trial was conversation topic number one at most social gatherings, business meetings, cocktail parties, political events, church gatherings, golf and bridge games—you name it.

Often it has been observed that humanity has learned its greatest lessons from its most challenging times. One of the enduring and endearing qualities of fair-minded people is that, if presented with the facts and given the opportunity, they can judge right from wrong—and when necessary, alter their opinion in the interest of the common good.

While the case against George Bush was yet to be decided, at a minimum it sent a message that heads of governments, small and large, could no longer fight wars without having to face the considered opinion of citizens around the world.

It was customary for both the prosecution and defense teams to meet frequently during the course of a trial. Much needed to be discussed, including an analysis of what had transpired and a debate about the attack going forward. Late in the evening of an already very long day, the defense team assembled inside the ICC defense conference room. Ed White spoke as he entered. "Just got off the phone with Don Rumsfeld. He's not coming."

Jonathan Ortloff looked up from a note he was writing. "What? George W. Bush's secretary of defense refuses to come to the defense of his commander in chief? Interesting."

Ed shrugged. "He said Condoleezza did a great job and Tommy Franks and George know everything he knows. 'Known knowns,' he said, and didn't want to be redundant."

Meredith Lott shook her head. "The truth is he doesn't want to come to The Hague because he could get arrested and put on trial for his advocacy of that war."

Jonathan added, "Same could be said for Condoleezza Rice, but she had the guts to come."

As arch as the comments were, they were also true. Just as Bush had been abducted and brought to the ICC to stand trial for his role in the Iraq War, the same fate could await both Rice and Rumsfeld should they venture outside the United States.

"Good point," Ed agreed. "Put your finger too close to the fire and you get burned."

Meredith nodded. "Well, we probably saved ourselves a whole bunch of 'unknown unknowns' and other such gobbledygook."

"Okay, Ms. Lott, what's your take on the status of the case so far?"

"The prosecution is strong, but they stray off base when they focus on *why* George fought the war and not *that* he fought it. The crimes are on trial here, not the reasons for the crimes. I think we should let them go on their merry way—give them enough rope to hang themselves."

"Agreed," Jonathan said. "I also think McBride is too strident. The judges clearly don't like his attitude, nor do they appreciate him badgering the witnesses. He lets his personal passions get the better of him."

Meredith agreed, "No kidding, he's a loose cannon."

The room was quiet for a moment before Ed asked the question everyone was thinking. "So, it has to be asked—should we advise George to testify in his own defense?"

"I say no," Jonathan shot back. "From day one, George's entire posture has been to dismiss the Court's credibility. Putting him on the stand will only undermine that position and possibly even legitimize the proceedings."

"That may be true," Meredith added, "but we have to remember he's fighting for his freedom—maybe for his life—if he's found guilty and his sentence is long enough. Fighting for what he believes in is what the world has come to expect from George W. Bush, and certainly what Americans expect of him. The strength that he showed as a decisive leader after 9/11 is exactly what we need him to project here and now. For George to sit there and do nothing, say nothing—would betray his very image, not to mention his legacy."

Ed nodded. "I think you're right. It's just not his style to sit back passively, no matter the odds or how severe the consequences."

"But what about command responsibility?" Jonathan countered. "The prosecution will try to tie George as commander in chief to all war crimes committed during the Iraq War."

"We'll have to counter that," Meredith challenged. "Even though he was president and commander in chief, he was several organizational layers above those who were actually making the decisions on the ground that led to those atrocities."

Ed started to pace. "Yes, George will have to make the point continually and forcefully that he did what he did to protect and defend the security of the American people—and for the betterment of the Iraqi society—maybe even the security of the entire Middle East."

Jonathan became more animated. "But won't that just open the door for McBride and Shadid to implicate the neoconservative thinking of Cheney, Rumsfeld, Wolfowitz, and others who may have conspired with George to wage war in the first place?"

Meredith countered: "Maybe so, but if it did, it would confuse and complicate their case and ultimately damage their chances of winning."

They all were noodling the question until Ed looked from Jonathan to Meredith and asked, "Okay, people, guts-ball here. We have to decide: Do we ask George to testify?"

"I say yes," Meredith quickly responded. "I think he would be a forceful voice in his own defense, maybe even critical."

"Jonathan?"

"I say no. It's a risk we don't have to take—too many traps. They can't get to George unless *we* put him on the stand."

Ed countered. "But not putting him on the stand could be the very thing that loses the case for us. George W. Bush is who he is. If he's going down, he's not going down without a fight. He's got to go down swinging. I need to discuss this with George and Laura. It's their lives that are at stake."

At the same time the defense team was meeting, Michael and Nadia were strolling along a sidewalk in a light drizzle. The lights of the city seen through the gauze of drizzle gave each scene a vague impressionistic quality. Eventually, Nadia asked, "So, you think we're winning?"

"I always think we're winning."

"So sure of yourself?"

"Comes from my mother, for better or worse."

"How so?"

"Every night when I was a young boy my mother tucked me into bed and told me how special I was. Mothers . . . you know."

"Not all mothers, unfortunately." They walked a few more steps in silence before Nadia asked, "What do you worry about?"

"That it's not what you or I think or say that matters. It's the majority judgment of one man from Great Britain, one woman from Japan, and one man from Nigeria. We can advocate all we want, but all that matters in the end is what they think."

"Seems like Bush can't help his own case if he doesn't testify."

"Yeah, well, he doesn't have to."

"I think he's dead in the water if he doesn't."

"I think he's dead in the water if he *does*."

"Really? You think that?"

Michael stopped and turned to Nadia for emphasis. "If Bush swears to tell the truth, which he'll have to, the truth will bury him."

"So, you *want* him to testify?"

"Yes, and we will nail him to the wall."

They stood in the drizzle under the umbrella studying each other at close range before Michael added, "If leaders of super-powers get away with waging unnecessary wars with impunity—then humankind is doomed to have more such wars. Simple."

"And fatalistic."

"Guilty as charged."

Later that night, as the drizzle turned into heavy rain, George and Laura Bush sat alone in a detention center meeting room. Laura asked, "How do you think the witness testimony went?"

George shrugged. "Okay, I guess. In any war there's always a lot of collateral damage. Easy to find people who were damaged."

"We need to bring in more people who benefited from the war. No one is talking much about the fact that Iraq is now a democracy."

"This is not as much about humanity or politics as it is about the strict application of international laws."

"Did you ever think you'd be held accountable to those laws?"

"No, I didn't. Neither did other presidents before me."

"George, Ed left a message about wanting to discuss the possibility of you testifying."

"I've been thinking about it."

"Nobody knows more about what you did and why you did it than you. George, you're not a criminal and you're not a murderer. It's just not who you are."

"Here's what I do know: If I don't testify and I am found guilty, it would be horrible—really horrible for all of us. I could never live with myself if I didn't at least *try* to defend myself."

"You're a pretty convincing guy when you put your mind to it."

"I couldn't bear the thought of having you, and our daughters, and our extended families, and the American people suffer the shame of me being found guilty."

"So let's go fight it."

Less than thirty minutes later, Laura Bush sat in a lounge chair in her suite engaged in one of the most important conversations of her life. Ed White was pacing. "Both George and you need to understand that this could be the make-or-break decision of the entire trial."

Laura replied, "We understand, but in our heart of hearts we think it is the right thing to do."

"So, he's willing to testify?"

"Yes. He was already considering it. He's willing to testify if you agree it's the right thing to do."

"Honestly, Laura, my team is conflicted. Meredith favors it. Jonathan is opposed."

Studying White carefully, Laura asked, "And you, Ed—what do you think?"

This was the very question Ed White had wrestled with since he first heard about his friend's abduction. In the mix and balance of legal discourse, there was no right answer, as it would depend on many unknowable variables, most especially what was going on in the minds of the judges. The matter was always going to be a game-day decision, and that day had arrived.

Ed took Laura's hand. "I have these two thoughts. If in his and your heart of hearts, it is the right thing to do, then it is the right thing to do. And then you and George, and all of us who love him should never look back. As for me, if our plan is to do everything we can to win the case, then he should testify. Period. End of statement."

CHAPTER FOURTEEN

In Search of the Truth

The truth is incontrovertible.
Panic may resent it, ignorance may deride it,
malice may attack it, but in the end, there it is.
—Winston Churchill

Following the decision that George Bush would testify, his defense attorneys requested a one-week recess of the trial in order to prepare the defendant for testimony. Consistent with customary legal protocol, the request was granted. Concurrently the prosecutors were informed, and this set in motion a flurry of preparation by both teams of attorneys.

The world's press of course was not thrilled with the delay and spent the next week in hot debate about the wisdom of Bush's decision to testify.

Finally the most important day of what was now being labeled "The Trial of the Century" had arrived. Tens of thousands of people from all over the world assembled outside the ICC building, either to root for George Bush's innocence or to clamor for his guilt. Inside, the courtroom was jam-packed and the public gallery was standing room only. Laura Bush was escorted into the public gallery and discreetly led to an aisle seat in the back row.

Presiding judge Harrison Hurst-Brown announced and gaveled the case back in session and then invited the defense to call its next witness.

Ed White stood and pronounced with all due gravity, "Thank you, Your Honor. The defense wishes to call to the witness bench the forty-third president of the United States, Mr. George W. Bush."

As he walked to the witness bench, George Bush looked only at the three ICC judges who would determine his fate. He displayed the supreme confidence of Muhammad Ali entering the ring before a heavyweight championship fight he knew he would win.

Judge Hurst-Brown asked Bush to raise his right hand and read the swearing-in document, which he did in a clear and confident voice: "I, George W. Bush, solemnly declare that I will speak the truth, the whole truth, and nothing but the truth."

Hurst-Brown said, "Thank you, Mr. Bush. Defense may commence with its questioning."

Then Bush's longtime friend from Texas, Ed White, smiled at him warmly and began, "Mr. President, thank you for your willingness to testify."

"Very much my pleasure."

White started methodically. "Following the war in Kuwait that your father, President George H. W. Bush, waged so effectively, UN Resolution 687 required Saddam Hussein to destroy his military arsenal. Can you inform us of what he actually did?"

"Sure. Resolution 687 banned Iraq from possessing biological, chemical, or nuclear weapons or the means to produce them. To ensure compliance, Saddam was required to submit to a UN monitoring and verification system. At first, Saddam claimed he had only a limited stockpile of chemical weapons and Scud missiles. Over time, UN inspectors discovered a vast arsenal of weapons. Saddam had filled thousands of bombs and warheads with chemical agents. He had a weapons program that was about two years away from yielding a nuclear bomb."

White pressed on: "The prosecution has spent a lot of time focusing on the reason why the Iraq War should not have been fought. Can you tell us why it *should have* been fought?"

"We believed Saddam's weakness was that he loved power and would do anything to keep it. If we could convince him we were serious about removing his regime, there was a chance he would stop producing WMD, end his advocacy of terror, stop harassing his neighbors, and over time, respect the fundamental human rights of his people. The odds of success were long, but given the alternative, it was worth the effort."

"And can you share with us your strategy?"

"First, I wanted to rally a coalition of nations to make clear that Saddam's defiance of international obligations was unacceptable. Then, I wanted to develop a credible military option that could be used if he failed to comply. These tracks would run parallel at first, but if the military option became necessary, the tracks would converge. That would be the moment of decision, and ultimately it would be Saddam's to make."

"The 9/11 attacks obviously had a huge effect on all of us. Explain why 9/11 caused you to focus specifically on Saddam Hussein."

"Before 9/11, Saddam was a problem America might have been able to manage. But post-9/11 my view changed. I had just witnessed the damage inflicted by nineteen fanatics, armed with nothing more than box cutters. I could only imagine the destruction possible if an enemy dictator gave his WMD to terrorists. The stakes were too high to trust a ruthless dictator given the current evidence available. The lesson of 9/11 was that if we waited for a danger to fully materialize, we waited too long."

Observing that his friend and client was more than up to the task, Ed White amped up the intensity. "You repeatedly targeted Saddam Hussein as an enemy of the United States and other friendly countries in the world. Other than your own personal feelings, what evidence did you have that led you to focus on him specifically?"

"He was a sworn enemy of the United States. He'd fired at our aircraft, praised 9/11, and even tried to assassinate my father. Saddam didn't just violate trivial international demands; he defied sixteen UN resolutions dating back to the nineties. He didn't just rule brutally; he and his henchmen tortured innocent people, raped female political opponents in front of their families, scalded dissidents with acid, and dumped tens of thousands of Iraqis into mass graves. Saddam decreed that people who criticized him would have their tongues cut out."

"During the buildup to the Iraq War, and certainly in these proceedings thus far, much has been said about weapons of mass destruction. Would you please set the record straight about Saddam Hussein's possession of WMD and perhaps other biological and chemical weapons as well?"

"Absolutely. Saddam didn't just have WMD; he *used* them. He deployed mustard gas and nerve agents against the Iranians and massacred more than five thousand innocent Iraqi people in a chemical attack on the Kurdish village of Halabja. The problem was, nobody knew what Saddam had done with his biological and chemical stockpiles, especially after he had booted the weapons inspectors out of his country. After reviewing the information available at the time, many intelligence agencies around the world came to the same conclusion I did: Saddam had WMD and the capacity to produce more."

"And you were in constant communication with Secretary of State Colin Powell?"

"Yes. Neither of us wanted war. I told Colin that while I was hopeful diplomacy would work, it was possible we would reach a point where war was the only option we had. I asked if he would support military action as a last resort. He said, 'If this is what you have to do, I'm with you, Mr. President.'"

"You were also in close communication with Prime Minister Tony Blair. You and he agreed to seek a UN resolution to demonstrate support and solidarity from the rest of the world regarding your concerns about Saddam and Iraq."

George Bush seemed to relish the chance to tell his story to both the Court and the worldwide audience he knew would be watching. "Correct. We told the UN delegation that the world was facing a test and that the United Nations was at a crucial and defining moment. I posed the question: Are UN Security Council resolutions to be honored and enforced, or to be cast aside without consequence? Will the UN serve its purpose or will it be rendered irrelevant? We needed nine of the fifteen Security Council members without a veto from France, Russia, or China. The vote was unanimous, fifteen to zero, including Great Britain, France, Russia, China, and Syria. The world was on record: Saddam had a final opportunity to comply with his obligation to disclose and disarm."

"And if he didn't?"

"He would face 'serious consequences.' Under UN Security Council Resolution 1441, Iraq had thirty days to submit a current, accurate, and complete declaration of all WMD-related programs. The resolution made clear that the burden of proof rested with Saddam. The inspectors did not have to prove that *he had* weapons. He had to prove that *he did not.*"

"But Saddam never did provide conclusive evidence that he was in compliance with the UN's demand for transparency."

"No, sir, he did not. When he submitted his report, Hans Blix, who led the UN inspections, called it 'rich in volume but poor in information.' Saddam was continuing his pattern of deception. The only way to keep the pressure on him would be to present evidence ourselves. I asked CIA director Tenet to brief me on what intelligence we could declassify that would prove Saddam had WMD. Tenet assured me we had sufficient evidence, saying, 'It's a slam dunk.' That's what he said—'a slam dunk.' And I believed him. I'd been receiving intelligence briefings on Iraq for years. The conclusion that Saddam possessed WMD had universal consensus. My predecessor, Bill Clinton, believed it. Republicans and Democrats on Capitol Hill believed it. Intelligence agencies in Germany, France, Great Britain, Russia, China, and Egypt believed it."

"And as Saddam showed no interest in complying with UN demands, it made it more apparent than ever that he had something to hide."

Sensing the momentum growing in his favor, Bush turned on a bit of his well-known charm. "Exactly. It became increasingly clear that my prayer for peace would not be answered. Saddam appeared not to have come to a genuine acceptance of the disarmament that was demanded of him. In retrospect, of course, we all should've pushed harder on the intelligence and revisited our assumptions a little more. But at the same time, the evidence and logic pointed in the other direction. I asked myself, if Saddam didn't have WMD, why on earth would he subject himself to a war he would almost certainly lose?"

"As president of the United States, did you feel you had both the moral and legal authority to wage the Iraq War?"

"Yes, sir, I did, and still do. The US Constitution vests the president with executive power. That power reaches its zenith when wielded to protect national security. Both the United States Congress and the United Nations provided the legal and moral authority necessary to wage the war. No debate about that."

White let those words hang in the room for a moment before continuing: "Mr. Bush, you've been accused of war crimes. But in truth you were only trying to protect and defend the citizens of the United States, which you were elected to do."

"I was trying in the best way I knew how. The fundamental questions I know people ask are whether or not we won that war—whether or not democracy won and will it take hold in Iraq? And will it change people's attitudes in the future? I believe it will. History has proven that democracies can change societies. The classic case I like to cite is Japan. Prime Minister Koizumi is one of my best friends. I find it interesting that he joined me as a peacemaker on a variety of issues, and yet my father fought the Japanese in World War II, when Japan was a sworn enemy of the United States. Today Japan is an ally of peace. And what took place? Well, what took place was a Japanese-style democracy."

"Thank you, Mr. President." White turned confidently to the ICC judges and said, "No further questions at this time, Your Honors."

"Thank you, Mr. White," Hurst-Brown said and then turned to the prosecution table. "Prosecution may proceed with cross-examination."

And just like that, after more than a year of research, investigation, preparation, and planning, the moment for Michael McBride to hold George W. Bush accountable for the war crimes of which he was accused had arrived.

"Thank you, Your Honors," McBride said confidently and turned to confront the defendant. "Mr. Bush, I know you're a big sportsman and love to play games. So I'm going to lay out the rules of this game in case you don't know them. All crimes in international law require two elements. The first is criminal intent, referred to as 'mens rea.' Criminal intent must include elements such as malice aforethought, intention, and knowing.

"The second is the prohibited act, referred to as 'actus reus.' The prohibited acts in your case include willful killing, imprisonment, persecution, causing great bodily injury and suffering, extensive destruction of property not justified by military necessity, depriving prisoners of a fair trial, and torture—especially of prisoners, and the other crimes that have been provided to you and your defense counsel. While all these crimes are deplorable, I note in particular your culpability in connection with Iraqi prisoner abuse at the Abu Ghraib prison. Any person who knows the truth will know that the inhumane and illegal prisoner abuse used by American soldiers in your war caused more damage to America's reputation around the world than any other single event in its history.

"So the questions to be answered, Mr. Bush, in order to establish your guilt would be: First, did you as president of the United States and commander in chief of all military operations personally and directly *cause* the Iraq War to happen? Second, what were the *circumstances* of your war that led to the inevitable killing of human beings? And, third, what are the *consequences* of your war in terms of human lives lost, property damaged or destroyed, prisoner abuses, etcetera?"

McBride turned to the judges and looked each in the eye for a few seconds, no doubt to emphasize the universal and historic significance of the testimony about to be given, and then continued:

"Your Honors, no one was publicly advocating war with Iraq until the accused, George W. Bush, started talking about it. It all started with George Bush creating something out of nothing.

"We understand that waging a war is not in and of itself a war crime, but the human casualties and physical destruction of the Iraq war are indeed tantamount to the very definitions of war crimes. The basic premise is this: George Bush's armed conflict with Iraq lasted eight years and nine months, during which forty-five hundred American soldiers, three hundred and twenty coalition soldiers, a minimum of one hundred and fifty thousand Iraqi soldiers, and hundreds of thousands of innocent Iraqi citizens were murdered. All of this is to say that if it can be proven that the accused, George Bush, was the single person most responsible for causing the war to happen, and that war crimes were in fact committed, then he is criminally liable for those crimes."

That said, McBride began his questioning. "So, George W. Bush, to get you on the record at last, why did you take America to war with Iraq?"

Bush responded immediately and forcefully. "Following the attacks of 9/11, I made an important decision—the United States would consider any nation that harbored terrorists to be responsible for the acts of those terrorists. Specifically regarding Iraq, my position was that we should be optimistic that diplomacy and international pressure would succeed in disarming Saddam Hussein's regime. But we couldn't allow him to have weapons of mass destruction. I would not let that happen."

"Will you concede once and for all that Saddam Hussein did not have WMD in 2003, the year you started your war?"

"It's easy for you to arrogantly state now that he didn't have WMD. But if you were charged with protecting two hundred and ninety million Americans, and you *weren't sure he didn't have*

them—and that the last time you checked he *did* have them—
you wouldn't be so cocksure of yourself."

"Mr. Bush, on September 20, 2001, nine days after 9/11, you
said in a congressional address, 'Americans are asking who attacked
our country. The evidence all points to a collection of loosely affili-
ated terrorist organizations known as al Qaeda.' That's what you
said. So you knew it was al Qaeda that was responsible for the 9/11
attacks and Saddam Hussein had nothing to do with it?"

"We believed Saddam might have been in cahoots with al
Qaeda."

McBride had been waiting for years to ask this next question. "But in that speech nine days after 9/11, *you didn't mention Saddam even once.* You only mentioned al Qaeda, which as
everybody knew was founded and led by Osama bin Laden."

Bush shot back, "We went after al Qaeda. Most of them were
in Afghanistan. Less than a month after 9/11, in October 2001,
we started a war in Afghanistan. Our goals were to remove the
Taliban and destroy al Qaeda."

"According to your secretary of state, most of the ground
fighting was outsourced to Afghan warlords and security forces.
Why didn't you use the full force of the United States military to
bring the 9/11 perpetrators to justice?"

"We used the military strategy we thought best for the task,
especially given the physical challenges in Afghanistan and the
nature of the enemy."

"After trying unsuccessfully to get bin Laden, you eventually
dismissed him. In order to kill a snake you have to kill the head
of the snake."

"I didn't know if bin Laden was hiding in some cave somewhere or not. Deep in my heart I knew the man was on the run,
if he was even alive at all."

"But you didn't destroy al Qaeda, and you didn't take out bin Laden. So in that respect, you failed in your obligation to the American people to seek out and destroy the very people who committed the atrocities of 9/11. When bin Laden was spotted in the Tora Bora region, why didn't you take him out then?"

"Because terror is about more than one person," Mr. Bush answered, growing increasingly impatient. "The idea of focusing on one person indicates to me that people don't understand the scope of the mission."

"In an interview in the Oval Office, December 2001, three months after 9/11, you said we're going to 'get Osama bin Laden dead or alive. Either way, it doesn't matter to me.' If you would've done just that, we wouldn't be here today. Instead you turned to Saddam Hussein, who had never directly terrorized America, or Americans."

"Obviously, I judged Saddam, given his past record, to be a bigger problem at the time."

"Mr. Bush, respectfully I guess, that doesn't make any sense. There was no evidence that Saddam had WMD since the 1990s. If you were going to ignore al Qaeda and bin Laden and target another regime that was a problem, why not Bashar al-Assad in Syria? Or Kim Jong Il in North Korea? It would've made about the same amount of sense as targeting Saddam Hussein. Was it because you realized that bin Laden and al Qaeda would be a long, complicated fight, so you targeted Saddam instead because he was old and weak by then and you wanted to prove yourself a strong, decisive president, boldly responding to 9/11?"

"That is a ridiculous allegation. After 9/11, I had to send a clear message to other terrorist organizations around the world that they couldn't attack America and get away with it. They had to pay the price. You obviously don't understand the geopolitical realities of the time."

McBride snapped back, "One of us doesn't, that's for sure."

The exchange had gotten personal. The air crackled with the intensity.

McBride continued his assault. "The truth is you took America's thirst for revenge after 9/11, pivoted attention away from bin Laden, and directed it toward Saddam. The initial reason you gave for invading Iraq was that Saddam had WMD and posed an imminent threat to the security of the United States.

"Mr. Bush, this brings us to a critically important issue in this proceeding—*what you knew and when you knew it*. I call your attention to the declassified Joint Chiefs of Staff INR intelligence report entitled 'Iraq: Status of WMD Programs' that was circulated in September 2002, *six months before you ordered the invasion of Iraq*. Under oath and in plain view of all peace-loving peoples of the world, George Bush, did you receive that report?"

"As president, I received many intelligence reports from many sources."

"Were you apprised of the details contained in that Joint Chiefs' report?"

"I just said I got many reports. I couldn't possibly remember the specific details of each."

"Did you read or were you made aware of the following intel regarding Iraq's military capabilities that were contained in that report: 'Our knowledge of the Iraqi weapons program *is based largely, perhaps 90 percent, on analysis of imprecise intelligence*'?"

White interrupted, "Objection, Your Honors! Badgering the witness."

Hurst-Brown responded immediately, "Objection overruled. Prosecution may continue."

Breaking protocol, defense attorney White interrupted again, this time to offer legal advice to his friend. "George, you don't have to answer these questions."

Undeterred, McBride ratcheted up the pressure. "More from the Joint Chiefs' report: 'Our assessments *rely heavily on analytic assumptions and judgment rather than hard evidence.* We *do not know with confidence* the location of any nuclear-weapon-related facilities. We *cannot confirm the identity of any Iraqi facilities* that produce, test, fill, or store biological weapons.' Furthermore, both UN and US weapons inspectors scouring Iraq before the war came to the same conclusion: Saddam *did not possess WMD*, having disposed of them after the Gulf War in 1991. The question is, George Bush, *when you alleged that Saddam had WMD, were you cherry-picking the facts or were you outright lying?*"

"There were as many intelligence experts that thought Saddam had WMD as not. I was not going to play Russian roulette with the lives of the American people."

"Tragically, the allegation that Saddam had WMD became the basis of the misleading propaganda you started force-feeding Congress and the American people—the facts according to George W. Bush."

"People have different recollections of history. It depended on which intelligence sources you believed and what your point of view was."

"Nonsense. The truth is the truth. If no one could prove he had WMD, and he hadn't had them for more than a decade . . . *then he didn't have them!*"

Bush offered no comment. The two equally intent and forceful combatants just glared at each other. McBride continued, "After your allegations that Saddam had WMD *were proven false*, and everybody knew Saddam was not then and had never been a direct threat to the security of the United States, you changed your tune and started to advocate that coalition forces should free the Iraqi people and thus allow free elections, which would lead to democracy in Iraq."

"Our belief was that if Iraq could become a democracy, other countries in the region might follow."

"So even though the majority of Muslim-based Middle Eastern countries had not embraced democracy for thousands of years, George Bush, early in the twenty-first century, after having ravaged the country of Iraq with eight and a half years of war, was hoping they would magically embrace democracy?"

Bush looked insulted by such a condescending assertion and punched back, "Germany embraced democracy after World War II."

With even more venom, McBride counterpunched, "Germany was not a Muslim country. And the Allied powers basically made democracy a condition of surrender." Sensing Bush was vulnerable, McBride quickly continued. "If you had said when you first started your drumbeat for war that it was to provide Iraqis with free elections, you knew Americans would never have bought that as a justification for invading Iraq. Americans are not stupid. If that was reason enough for going to war, during the past fifty years America would have been fighting wars all over the world: China, Iran, North Korea, Cambodia, Darfur, Myanmar, Cuba, just to name a few. The fact is that the majority of member states in the United Nations disapproved of your war."

"Many world leaders shared my assessment of the threat Iraq posed: Tony Blair of the UK, John Howard of Australia, José María Aznar of Spain, Junichiro Koizumi of Japan, Jan Peter Balkenende of the Netherlands, Anders Fogh Rasmussen of Denmark, and most other leaders in Central and Eastern Europe."

McBride countered, "However, France, Germany, Russia, China, and the majority of member nations in the UN refused to go along with your obsession to wage that war."

"France had significant economic interest in Iraq. I was not surprised when President Chirac cautioned against using military force against Iraq. If you checked the facts, Mr. McBride, you would see that Iraq purchased something like twenty-five billion dollars' worth of military equipment from France. The problem with Chirac's logic was that without the credible threat of force, diplomacy would be toothless and Saddam Hussein would escape the scrutiny of the free world once again."

"But the reality is that France never opposed war with Iraq; it only opposed your mad rush to war. President Chirac knew it would enrage Arabic and Islamic public opinion and, as he said, 'create a large number of little bin Ladens.' In a joint interview with CBS and CNN on March 16, 2003, four days before you invaded Iraq, Mr. Chirac said, 'We feel there is another option, another more normal way, a less dramatic way than war. And we should pursue it until we have come to a dead end.' Russia opposed your war as well?"

"Putin didn't consider Saddam a threat and didn't want to jeopardize Russia's lucrative oil contracts with Iraq."

McBride was relentless. "German chancellor Gerhard Schröder denounced the use of force against Iraq. His justice minister said, 'Bush wants to divert attention from domestic political problems. Hitler also did that.'"

"That was bullshit. Hard to think of anything more insulting than being compared to Hitler by a German official."

McBride picked up a binder of documents he would refer to frequently. "In your first State of the Union address, January 29, 2002, you spoke of preventing, and I quote, 'regimes that sponsor terror from threatening America or her friends with weapons of mass destruction.' You mentioned North Korea and Iran, and then said, 'Iraq continues to flaunt its hostility toward America and to support terror. States like these constitute an axis of evil arming to threaten the peace of the world.' So, just four months after 9/11, when Americans wanted justice for the terrorists responsible for the attack, you started targeting North Korea, Iran, and Iraq. Why?"

"Because I was focused on the regimes I thought represented the greatest threat to America and her allies at the time."

"For the record, Mr. Bush, *not one* of the countries in your 'axis of evil' has lifted a finger to harm America or endanger the peace of the world years after you threatened they would. But back to the question, which I am going to keep asking until we get a coherent answer, four months after the 9/11 attacks— which Iraq had nothing to do with—why did you switch the attention from al Qaeda and bin Laden to Saddam Hussein?"

"Saddam had plotted to develop anthrax, nerve gas, and nuclear weapons for over a decade. He had used poison gas to murder thousands of his own citizens. His was a regime that agreed to international inspections and then kicked out the inspectors. This was a regime that had something to hide from the rest of the world."

"But it has been proven repeatedly that Saddam didn't have anything to hide. Inspectors were given access to every site they asked to visit. Hans Blix said, and I quote, 'On no particular occasion were we denied access.' In total, UN and US inspectors conducted more than nine hundred inspections at over five hundred sites *and found nothing.*"

No response from Bush. McBride continued, "In addition to allowing unfettered inspections, Saddam had done nothing to harm or threaten the United States or its allies since the 1990s, more than a decade before the time in question. In your second State of the Union address, January 29, 2003, you *again* pivoted away from bin Laden and al Qaeda, saying, 'We have called on the United Nations to fulfill its charter and stand by its demand that *Iraq* disarm.' Iraq? In that speech you didn't mention Osama bin Laden or al Qaeda even once, but incredibly mentioned Iraq *five times* and Saddam Hussein *thirty-one times*. How could that be?"

"There was some ambiguity in the international community about Hussein, and I wanted to clear it up. Either he would come clean about his WMD or there would be war."

"You then moved this bait and switch of yours to the international stage with desperate scaremongering and dire warnings. In your speech to the UN General Assembly, September 12, 2002, you described Iraq as 'a grave and gathering danger.' Then, again, falsely creating the impression that Iraq had something to do with 9/11, you said, 'The attacks of September 11 would be a prelude to far greater horrors.' Again the question, why Saddam Hussein and not bin Laden . . . al Queda and not Iraq?"

Bush was running out of patience. "I told you; I didn't know where bin Laden was. We were going after al Qaeda at large. I was truly not concerned about bin Laden. I knew he was on the run. But once we set out our policy and started executing the plan, we shoved him more and more to the margins."

"And eventually turned your total focus to war with Iraq?"

"Yes, because, as I said, that's where I determined the greatest threat to be. Leadership must utilize estimates and opinions of top military advisors to make the tough decisions necessary to protect their country. There is hardly ever a decision that is 100 percent right or 100 percent wrong. You're always dealing with percentages of the optimum, seeking to find the best possible outcome in the situation you're confronted with."

Mr. Bush sat back with a smug expression, presumably because he calculated that while he may not have won this critically important exchange, he didn't lose it either.

McBride, evidencing both frustration and anger, pressed on. "Mr. Bush, without an acceptable answer to this central question, we're going to leave this issue to the judgment of the three judges, and perhaps the people around the world who are following this case, and maybe even historians who will look back upon this case in the future."

McBride shuffled through some papers and started a new offensive. "Okay, next question: Why your incredible rush to war? The UN inspectors were making good progress and Saddam was giving them unlimited access. Why the rush? Surely you didn't think Saddam would launch a nuclear attack on the United States while UN and US inspectors were swarming all over his country. And WMD, if he had any—which he didn't—have a maximum strike range of ninety miles. Iraq is half the circumference of the world away from the United States. On top of that, one of your top generals, Anthony Zinni, was saying at the time that containment was 'working remarkably well.'"

"For more than a year, I had tried to address the threat from Saddam Hussein without going to war. We obtained a UN resolution making it clear there would be serious consequences if he continued to defy us. I gave Saddam and his sons forty-eight hours to avoid war. He rejected every opportunity. The only logical conclusion was that he did have something to hide, something so important that he was willing to go to war to conceal it. I knew the consequences my order would bring. But letting a sworn enemy of America refuse to account for his weapons of mass destruction was a risk I could not afford to take."

McBride turned to address the judges. "Your Honors, I'd like to call your attention to the sentence George Bush just said regarding his knowing the consequences his orders would bring, and request the court reporter read back that exact sentence, starting with 'I knew.'"

Hurst-Brown instructed the court reporter to read the sentence. She backed up her dictation machine to the exact point and began, "I knew the consequences my order would bring. But letting a sworn enemy of America refuse to account for his weapons of mass destruction was a risk I could not afford to take."

"Thank you," McBride said. "Your Honors, the sentence is evidence of George Bush's malice aforethought, which is required to prove criminal intent."

He turned back to Bush. "You knew Saddam Hussein did not have the military capacity to attack the United States at the time in question. Here's the proof: On December 28, 2002, three months before your war, General Franks compared Iraq's state of combat readiness in 1991, the beginning of the Gulf War, to its combat readiness in 2003, the beginning of your war. We'll use this chart for clarity, and note it is submitted as Prosecution Evidence #5."

The ICC judges and all others turned their attention to the screens in the courtroom or the chart that was provided in the binder of evidence. McBride read the chart verbatim:

Iraq Military Capability, 1991 vs. 2003

- Men in uniform: 1991—over one million. 2003—three hundred fifty thousand.
- Divisions consisting of more than ten thousand soldiers: 1991—sixty-eight. 2003—twenty-three.

- Tanks: 1991—six thousand. 2003—two thousand six hundred.
- Rocket launchers and guns: 1991—four thousand. 2003— two thousand seven hundred.

"Quite aside from the fact that Iraq had reduced capacity, America had grown much stronger. Quoting General Franks, 'Not only is Iraq's military smaller than what it was in 1991, but advances in America's precision weapons and command make our forces now much more capable than they were then.' Not only did Iraq have virtually zero capacity to attack the United States; it had very little capacity to defend itself."

McBride paused to allow the facts to register, and continued his attack. "And so, knowing all that, for the love of God, why were you in such a rush? Why didn't you just wait, as many world leaders pled with you to do, and let UN inspectors take another few weeks to complete their inspections? Not months, but a few weeks?"

With obvious disdain, Bush countered, "Three months before the invasion, Tony Blair and I agreed that Saddam had violated the UN Security Council resolution by submitting a false declaration. We had ample justification to enforce the 'serious consequences' provision in Resolution 1441. We had experienced the horror of September 11. We had seen that those who hate America were willing to crash airplanes into tall buildings full of innocent people. We couldn't afford to wait."

"You couldn't afford to wait? Really? Couldn't afford to wait a few weeks—or couldn't control your near hysterical obsession to get Saddam Hussein?"

White interjected, "Objection, Your Honor. False accusation. Badgering the witness."

"Objection sustained."

McBride nodded to Hurst-Brown and continued, "Mr. Bush, since you and your closest advisors never fought in a war—not Dick Cheney, not Don Rumsfeld, and not Condoleezza Rice—and with so many experienced military minds in America pleading for restraint, did you ever stop to consider you could accomplish your goals without having to send America's sons and daughters to fight a massively destructive war?"

McBride had touched a sensitive nerve. Bush shot back in anger, "This line of questioning is a bunch of crap. I was in constant communication with my Joint Chiefs of Staff. The overwhelming consensus was that we had to engage in the war to obtain our stated objectives."

Sensing Bush was losing his composure, McBride attacked with increased intensity. "No, the truth is that going to war *was not* the overwhelming consensus of the US military *until you convinced them you were going to war* and, out of respect for the presidency and loyalty to duty, they went along with you. They did *what you made them do* as their commander in chief.

"Besides, there's a difference between the military and the leader of the nation, whose job it is to gain the greatest advantage while sacrificing the least in terms of lives lost, money spent, and damage to civilization. Presidents Eisenhower, Kennedy, Reagan, and Clinton all knew that dealing with adversaries across the negotiating table was a better way to promote America's values and improve security than resorting to war. Those presidents understood that fair-minded, tough diplomacy and economic sanctions were strengths, not weaknesses, and that exhausting diplomatic options *before sending troops into battle* was a fundamental responsibility of leadership. The cost of your departure from those basic concepts of human decency reverberates around the world even to this day."

"You have a far too simplistic view of world diplomacy and, frankly, I think a dangerous one. You don't negotiate with proven terrorists like Saddam Hussein."

"You also don't attack the elected president of a sovereign country and remove him just because you don't like him. In your televised address March 17, 2003, three days before your war, you said: 'Intelligence gathered by this and other governments leaves no doubt that the Iraq regime continues to possess and conceal some of the most lethal weapons ever devised.' That was not true, as has been proven. You continued, 'Responding to such enemies only after they have struck is not self-defense; it is suicide. The security of the world requires disarming Saddam Hussein now.'"

Bush seemed ready to engage in this fight and countered aggressively, "Two months before the invasion, Hans Blix told the United Nations that his inspectors had discovered warheads that Saddam had failed to declare or destroy, and they found indications of the highly toxic VX nerve agent, which is used to make mustard gas. The Iraqi government was defying the inspections process. It had violated Resolution 1441 by blocking U-2 flights and hiding three thousand documents in the home of an Iraqi nuclear official."

"It is astonishing," McBride opined, "how the intel you used was at such variance with most other US government intelligence sources and her allies. Can we agree at least that the intel from both US and international sources was conflicted?"

"Yes."

"No one could know for certain what Saddam's capacity was at that time?"

"Presidents have to make tough decisions based on the intel they receive. That's what I did as the duly elected president and commander in chief."

"But your decision to wage war with Iraq was nothing more than a calculated risk based on your interpretation of conflicting intel. Factored into that calculation needed to be the risk of being wrong! Human lives—many of them—were at stake. Sons and daughters of American families would be killed by the thousands. George Bush, if your calculation would've included sending your daughters to war, would you have been so willing to commit American troops?"

White jumped out of his seat. "Objection, Your Honor. Not relevant."

"Objection overruled."

Bush glared at the prosecutor. "Watch yourself, McBride."

McBride ignored him. "You must've known Saddam had only engaged in regional wars with his neighbors—Iran in the eighties and Kuwait in the nineties. He never invaded any other countries or really even threatened to invade any other countries. Not Israel. Not Saudi Arabia. And certainly not the United States."

"He invaded Israel. Get your facts right."

"He lobbed a couple of bombs at Israel. He never invaded with ground troops. Virtually every US administration before you had cooperated with repressive governments in the region, certainly including Saudi Arabia and Egypt. George Bush, let's set the record straight now and forever. Did you attack Iraq to protect Israel?"

"No matter how many times you ask, my answer to questions of that nature will be the same."

"To protect your personal friends and longtime family business associates in Saudi Arabia?"

Bush did not respond.

"To protect Middle East oil production critical to American businesses?"

Once again, no response from Bush.

"To gain revenge against Saddam for his attempt to kill your father?"

Finally, Bush responded. "All of the above, and to protect the American people from the threat of a known terrorist."

"But none of that required or justified a full-on war. If you were so concerned about Saddam Hussein, you could've just targeted him specifically—sent in Special Ops Forces and taken him out in a matter of days. Or was it that you knew a war with Iraq would be hugely expensive and thus hugely profitable for America's military-industrial complex?"

Sensing momentum shifting in his direction, the prosecuting attorney was content to let the question linger, until Ed White stood to rescue his client. "Objection, Your Honor. Conjecture."

"Overruled," Hurst-Brown said immediately. "Prosecution may continue."

Anxious to capitalize on his momentum, McBride quickly pressed forward. "For the record, in the first full year of your war, 2004, American taxpayers spent 542.4 billion dollars on defense, primarily funding your war. Your war in total cost Americans more than four trillion dollars. That's 't' as in 'trillion,' not 'b' as in 'billion.'"

"The cost of freedom is not cheap."

"Indeed not. And the corporations that supply the US military with guns and vehicles and protective armor and food, and so on—corporations like Lockheed Martin, Boeing, General Dynamics, Raytheon, Halliburton—made ungodly sums of money. Stock prices rose to new heights. Friends of yours who were fat cats got even fatter. The US economy boomed. All good news for your mid-war reelection campaign, which of course you won. And all of this insane profiteering was done at the cost of precious human lives."

"I resent that implication."

"Resent it all you want, but isn't it true?"

"If you believe in the universality of freedom, as I do, then you believe those of us who are free have an obligation to help free those who are not."

"You speak of freeing the Iraqi people. Which Iraqis were you referring to, and what were you freeing them from? Saddam was a Sunni. Most Sunnis were fairly content with him being president. But the country as a whole was not asking to be freed in any of the ways you wanted to free them. They wanted to create their own Iraq. To address this very subject, the prosecution requests permission to enter into evidence the written testimony of Iraq's first postwar minister of defense, Mr. Ali Allawi, as Prosecution Evidence #6."

Hurst-Brown looked over to approving nods from his fellow judges and replied, "Request granted."

"Thank you, Your Honors. Prosecution enters this as evidence. Ms. Shadid, please read the statement made by your fellow countryman regarding America's liberation of Iraq."

Shadid stood with document in hand. "Quoting Mr. Allawi: 'The overthrow of the regime that ruled Iraq was achieved in record time, no more than a few weeks of sporadic fighting. There were *no public cheers for democracy, no indications that this was a people hungering for the freedoms and liberties of the West.* The attacks on government property, the wanton burning of ministries, libraries, and even sports stadiums, the images of booty being carted off by frenzied crowds, somehow did not fit with the behavior of grateful people who had just been liberated from tyranny.'"

McBride picked up, "Thank you, Ms. Shadid," and turned his attention back to the former president. "Mr. Bush, any comment?"

"Saddam Hussein was a bully and a murderer. You can find plenty of people in Iraq who will tell you how thankful they are to be no longer living under his tyranny."

"Perhaps so, but there are many more Iraqis who would say that removing Saddam is one thing, but invading and occupying their country for years is another thing altogether—and something virtually none of them wanted.

"One of America's most famous and respected five-star Army generals, who later served as president, was Dwight Eisenhower. In his farewell address to the nation, he spoke of a deep-seated fear he had after World War II. Quoting President Eisenhower: 'In the councils of government we must guard against the acquisition of unwarranted influence, whether sought or unsought, by the military-industrial complex. The potential for the disastrous rise of misplaced power exists and will persist.' Mr. Bush, I'm sure you were aware of this concern?"

"Of course."

"But you chose to ignore it," McBride shot back.

Bush didn't take the bait and only glared back in return.

McBride continued his attack. "The United States Declaration of Independence begins, 'We hold these truths to be self-evident, that all men are created equal, that they are endowed by their creator with certain unalienable rights, that among these are life, liberty, and the pursuit of happiness.' Do you believe America's founding fathers intended that just for Americans or for all people?"

Defense attorney White objected again: "Your Honors, the prosecution is doing nothing more than spouting irrelevant American history, none of which has any bearing on this case."

Hurst-Brown answered, "Objection sustained."

"Your Honors," White persisted, "with respect, the defendant has been subjected to sustained questioning for a noticeably long period of time. In the interest of fair treatment of a former president of the United States, defense requests a recess until tomorrow."

McBride approached the bench. "Your Honors, prosecution objects to this request and pleads that recess is not granted. We are in the middle of cross-examination and there is much to cover."

"The Court recognizes the prosecution's objection to recess," Hurst-Brown replied, "but it also recognizes it is an appropriate time to recess." He rapped his gavel. "Defense request is granted. The Court is adjourned until tomorrow, oh nine hundred sharp, when we will reconvene for prosecution questioning."

CHAPTER FIFTEEN

Practice What You Preach

*A nation of sheep must in time beget
a government of wolves.*

—Bertrand de Jouvenel

ollowing the abrupt recess of the case, news organizations scrambled to get their reporters on camera to recap the dramatic developments of the day. As the case had generated a huge amount of interest from all corners of the world, the lineup of camera crews covering the story had grown to sixty-seven, representing virtually all of the world's top broadcasters. What follows is a sampling of the reports.

The BBC's Elizabeth Reynolds interviewed international criminal law expert Alexandra Portenko, originally from Moscow and now living in London. Ms. Reynolds began, "Today can only be described as a monumentally important day in the life of the International Criminal Court, as the first leader of a superpower to be tried by the Court was sworn in to testify."

Turning to her guest, she asked, "Ms. Portenko, what do you make of former president George W. Bush's testimony thus far?"

Ms. Portenko replied, "As for Mr. Bush, I can give him more than a passing grade. Not so, however, for the prosecuting attorney Michael McBride. He needs to stop attacking Bush personally and make the effort to connect him more specifically to war atrocities that occurred in Iraq on his watch. That is how to get a conviction in a court of international law: proving specific crimes were committed, not arguing theoretical generalities."

Ms. Reynolds continued, "Mr. Bush may be intentionally trying to lead the prosecution away from himself and put the now dead Saddam Hussein back on trial."

Ms. Portenko nodded. "If that's what he's trying to do, it is not only brilliant but it appears to be working. McBride is not drawing the necessary connections via legal theories such as 'command responsibility' between Bush and specific incidents of crimes, including the torture at the Abu Ghraib prison facility, to name but one example of many."

Iraq's Al Rasheed TV commentator, Omar Kassab, offered the following assessment: "As we watch the trial take place in The Hague today, it is interesting to note the public opinion of Mr. Bush in America during the Iraq War. When George W. Bush left office, he had the lowest approval rating of any president in American history: 22 percent. Regarding the way Mr. Bush handled the Iraq War, according to polls taken in America, 73 percent disapproved. Noting that the decision in the Bush case requires at least two of three judges to find him guilty, perhaps these polling results provide some insight as to how the ICC judges might rule. Perhaps not."

China's CCTV correspondent Cheng Lee Teoh commented, "Even though George W. Bush and his cabinet waged the Iraq War, it was pointed out that none of them had any firsthand experience in war combat. Mr. Bush himself, seeking to avoid the Vietnam War, served in the Texas Air National Guard but was suspended for failing to take an annual physical examination.

Vice President Cheney received special deferments during the Vietnam War and, as a result, avoided military service. It is hard to understand how government officials can lead the military effectively without ever having had firsthand military experience themselves. Such a thing would never happen in this country."

On opposite sides of the ICC building, the defense and prosecution teams were using the evening recess to meet and discuss the case.

In the defense meeting, Ed White politely reminded his client about optimum courtroom protocol. "George, you must remain consistent with your testimony. The prosecuting attorneys will try to catch you in a discrepancy to create the impression that other claims you've made are inaccurate."

Meredith Lott nodded and added, "You're doing well, George, but just state the facts—sparingly and simply. Don't feel you need to elaborate. It will make the prosecution's job even harder."

Jonathan Ortloff chimed in, "Also, regardless of what McBride says or does, try to avoid attacking him back. Yes, he is an arrogant and pretentious asshole, but if the judges sense hostility from you, it is possible they could make a subliminal deduction that your frustration comes from guilt rather than anger."

Meredith added, "Remember that we follow the prosecution with cross-examination. We will provide you with plenty of opportunity to state your case clearly and completely, and of course, advocate for your innocence."

"Most importantly," Ed emphasized, "we need to remain cognizant that the prosecution bears the burden of proof. If the evidence is circumstantial or parenthetical—or if the questioning is accusatory rather than fact-finding—it will hurt their chances of winning."

Bush observed, "I feel like a boxer getting instructions from his corner between rounds of a heavyweight fight."

Ed smiled reassuringly. "Sorry, George. It's just that there's a lot to cover. I would also urge you to start playing to the judges more. Try to establish more human being–to–human being contact. Look at them more. Maybe even smile at them once in a while like everything's going to be okay. After all, your fate will be determined by their collective opinion."

Concurrently, the prosecutors were deep into their own analysis. Michael McBride sat with his hands clasped behind his head and feet up on the table. Nadia Shadid was up pacing around the room while commenting on the case. "Bush seems like a petulant schoolboy trying to justify a substandard homework assignment to his teacher."

Michael added, "Ignorance is no excuse for breaking well-known laws."

"Yes, Michael," Nadia snapped back. "But you have to stop browbeating him."

He glanced at her, surprised at the rare rebuke. She pressed her point. "If the judges sense your frustration, they may regard it as a weakness in our case."

"Nonsense, Nadia. Bush has selective memory and repeats his same damn well-rehearsed bullshit over and over again. We have to attack that, or he gets away with it."

"No, we don't, Michael. We simply have to present the evidence. If we can establish the truth of what he did and said, the legal process will take its course and justice will be served." They studied each other for a moment before Nadia continued, "The judges are not stupid or blind or deaf, Michael, for God's sake. If they consider this case a personal vendetta between you and Bush, we don't stand a chance."

Michael unclasped his hands, took his feet off the table, and conceded, "You may be right."

"No 'maybe,' Michael. I *am* right!"

They had never experienced such acrimony. After a few awkward seconds, Nadia tried to soften the discordant mood. "Michael, tell me please—you seem to have such personal animosity for George Bush. Why is that?"

Michael wasn't sure. He'd never thought about it. "George was elected president on his family's good name. Without his father, no one would have thought for two seconds about George junior being president. And as president—after and because of 9/11, he had the highest popularity rating ever, but by the time he left office he had the second lowest—behind Harry Truman who dropped two atomic bombs on the Japanese. And if that's not enough, he stuck the next president, Barack Obama, with the worst recession since the Depression. Look, he never should have been president of the United States. In fact, it could be argued that his presidency preempted the chances for his younger brother, Jeb, who would have been a much better president."

"Are you done?"

"Not quite. He's also duplicitous. He says he's a Christian, reads scripture, prays every day, follows Jesus's teachings. Hell, Jesus would have wept if he had seen the death and destruction he caused."

Silence, while they stared at each other. Michael was surprised at how angry he had become, and then it dawned on him, "Nadia . . . here's my principal beef with George W. Bush: He has never taken responsibility for his war. In light of all that is now known about the Iraq War, he never admitted it was wrong, and never apologized."

Nadia reached over and put her hand on his shoulder. "Michael, I understand and obviously agree. But you admonished me about not letting personal passions interfere with the administration of justice."

"Yeah, well . . ."

"Then practice what you preach."

CHAPTER SIXTEEN

Back in the Saddle

Oh, what a tangled web we weave
when first we practice to deceive!
—Walter Scott

At nine o'clock sharp the next morning, presiding judge Harrison Hurst-Brown rapped his gavel to start the new day and proclaimed, "*The Prosecutor v. George W. Bush* is back in session. Prosecution cross-examination of the accused may continue."

Michael McBride replied, "Thank you, Your Honor," and then turned to the defendant and abruptly restarted his questioning. "Evidence that you were personally responsible for the Iraq War is that you didn't even bother to ask your vice president, Dick Cheney, or secretary of defense, Donald Rumsfeld, about going to war, did you?"

Bush replied immediately, "I didn't need to ask their opinion. If you were sitting where I sat, you could see pretty clearly what they were thinking."

"Surely you must have asked the most trusted and respected member of your cabinet, the only member of your administration who had fought in a war, Secretary of State Colin Powell?"

"No. I knew where Colin Powell stood. I didn't agree with him."

"The fact is, Mr. Bush, you were hell-bent on having your war regardless of what others thought."

"That's absurd. While the world is undoubtedly safer with Saddam gone, the reality is I sent troops into combat *based on intelligence*—intelligence that proved to be false."

Silence fell over the courtroom, as that was the first time Bush had admitted guilt of any kind. McBride remained silent, hoping he would say more, and sure enough he did. "That was a massive blow to our credibility, my credibility. That shook the confidence of the American people. No one was more shocked or angry than I was when we didn't find WMD. I had a sickening feeling in my stomach every time I thought about it. I still do."

McBride let the admissions resonate in the Court before throwing kerosene on the bonfire. "Mr. Bush, you just admitted that there were no WMD in Iraq and that the evidence you relied on was false. Do you think that that absolves you of any guilt in connection with your war?"

White had to interject and did. "Objection, Your Honors. Asking the witness to speculate."

"Objection sustained," Hurst-Brown replied.

McBride turned to address the only people in the world whose opinions mattered in determining guilt or innocence in the case. "Your Honors, as we know in international criminal law, in order to prove guilt, criminal intent at the time of the crime has to be proven. In law, the word 'intent' means 'the state of a person's mind that directs his or her actions toward a specific objective.' According to the admissions Mr. Bush just made: First, the intelligence he used was wrong, and second, there were no WMD. Let's consider that in connection with 'intent.' If Mr. Bush was intent on a fair and honest assessment of Saddam's present-time capability before committing human lives and his nation's treasury to armed warfare, he would have had to be certain the intelligence was accurate—not questionable, not debatable, not conflicted, not disputed, but certain. As has been proven repeatedly, the intelligence was most definitely questioned, debated, conflicted, and disputed, and he knew it.

"Your Honors, I would like to direct your attention to an interview the accused did with ABC's Diane Sawyer in December 2003, nine months into his war. Ms. Sawyer asked Mr. Bush to make a distinction between Saddam Hussein *having* WMD as opposed to the *possibility* he could acquire them. Mr. Bush said, 'What's the difference? If he were to acquire weapons, he would be the danger.'

"Please note carefully, he said, '*If he were to acquire* weapons.' That's what he said in a live television interview nine months into his war—'if he *were to acquire*.' Your Honors, George Bush just admitted that he waged his war, and kept fighting his war, *knowing Saddam did not actually have WMD.* He ordered his war to start only on the possibility Saddam had WMD. And if he didn't know for sure Saddam had WMD, then his 'intent' was to fight his war regardless of the lack of evidence. He knowingly lied to the American people, the United States Congress, and the UN. Their approvals were secured based on false accusations made by the accused. And without valid approvals from Congress and the UN, Mr. Bush's presidential order to fight his war was illegal, making his war a criminal act."

Bush erupted, "You can always take questions and answers and flip 'em and spin 'em out of context any way you want."

McBride ignored Bush's nonsequacious outburst and continued, "Your Honors, the evidence we've presented from before, during, and after the Iraq War proves without any doubt that the accused waged a tragically destructive war without the proper legal, ethical, or moral justification. Given the substantial loss of human lives, destruction of physical property, prisoner torture, and all the rest attendant to his war—to consider George Bush anything *other than guilty of war crimes* would be a gross misapplication of international law."

McBride took a few steps toward Bush and pointed at him. "The domino effect of this man's war is as follows. He removed Saddam from power and in the process upset the balance of power that had existed in the region for years. Next, his plan for creating a democracy in Iraq was never going to happen because the majority of Iraqis didn't want democracy. Finally, Muslim anger over his unnecessary and illegal war, coupled with his arrogant attempt to influence the beliefs of Islamic people that had existed for thousands of years, emboldened al Qaeda and spawned new terrorist groups, such as the Islamic State, also known as ISIS or Daesh, which basically hates everything about America and Americans. Mr. Bush, what do you think would have happened if you had taken out bin Laden and destroyed al Qaeda instead of invading Iraq? Do you ever stop to think how different the world would be if you had done that?"

Bush didn't respond.

McBride continued, "If you hadn't insisted on waging your war, more than a million people would still be alive today and tens of thousands would not be suffering from the physical or mental wounds caused by your war. And most probably an uneasy peace would still exist in the region."

Finally, Bush fought back. "What would've happened if we lost our nerve and Iraq had fallen to al Qaeda? You ever think about that?"

McBride countered, "That's an absurd question. It was al Qaeda you should have destroyed in the first place. After al Qaeda attacked America on September 11, 2001, if you had engaged the full power of the US military to take out al Qaeda and bin Laden, they would no longer have been a threat to any country—not the United States and certainly not Iraq. Perhaps, maybe even probably, there never would have been an Islamic State.

"Anybody in America with a clear perspective knows you railroaded your country into an unnecessary war. Senator Ted Kennedy said, 'Bush's distortions misled Congress into its war vote. No president of the United States should employ distortion of the truth to take the nation to war.' A *New York Times* editorial two years into your war stated, 'The president did not allow the American people, or even Congress, to have the information necessary to make reasoned judgments of their own.' A *New York Times*/CBS nationwide poll taken after your war showed that the majority of Americans believed you *intentionally misled* the nation to promote war.

"What you did, George Bush, is universally unpopular. But the question before the Court now is whether or not it was criminal. Do the crimes you personally committed constitute war crimes, as defined by international law? In this arena, these three judges will have to make the decision. But the majority of people around the world think they do, which makes you one of the worst criminals of our time, however unlikely that may seem to you."

The former president was visibly upset. He swallowed hard, looked away in anger, took a moment to compose himself, and shot back: "It is not a criminal act for a president to do what he was elected to do by the American people."

"Oh really? The American people elected you to send their sons and daughters to the other side of the world, and spend their treasury, to fight a needless, reckless, and illegal war?"

The entire proceeding came to a standstill. Nobody said a word for a long moment. Perhaps figuring he might have said something he shouldn't have, Bush changed the subject. "I might add for the record that for the seven remaining years I was president after the 9/11 attacks, there were no other terrorist attacks on the United States. You can find plenty of Americans who would say that stopping terrorist attacks was worth it, whatever the price. I made America a safer place, period. End of statement."

That comment seemed to reignite McBride. "I'd like to call your attention to a curious series of events. The last act of Bill Clinton's presidency was to sign a document that would have paved the way for the United States to become a member of the ICC. One of your first acts as president was to 'unsign' that agreement, effectively eliminating any chance of the United States joining the ICC. You obviously did that because you knew you would be engaging in acts during your presidency that would violate international laws and did not want to be subjected to ICC jurisdiction."

White had heard enough. "Objection, Your Honors. Attempting to prejudice the judges' opinion."

Hurst-Brown agreed. "Objection sustained."

McBride all but ignored the ruling and continued. "Ironically, you would be the last person to quarrel with the death penalty. As governor of Texas, you were a strong proponent of the death penalty. In fact, you had the highest execution rate of any governor in American history. You signed death warrants for all but one of one hundred and fifty-three prisoners, most of whom had killed only one single person."

White pushed back again. "Objection! Irrelevant to this case!"

Hurst-Brown agreed. "Objection sustained."

McBride moved on. "There is no reason, legal or otherwise, why you, George Bush, should not be prosecuted for the war crimes of which you are accused. We all know that no one is above the law. I trust you agree that includes presidents of the United States?"

For the first time, Bush agreed with McBride. "Correct, no man is above the law. But there's man's law and there's God's law."

McBride smiled faintly as though he had finally been given the opening he had been waiting for. "What does God say about you killing a million people?"

"What God says to me is none of your business."

"'Thou shalt not kill,' and 'Love thy neighbor.' Aren't those two of the most important commandments?"

"This is ridiculous. That was war."

"You say God personally told you to go to war?"

"Objection!" White exclaimed. "Badgering the witness."

"Objection overruled."

McBride increased the intensity. "Before you were president you delivered a sermon in church. Wearing a robe and standing in front of a choir, you said, 'I have a sense of calm knowing that the Bible's admonition, "Thy will be done," is life's guide.'"

"I was in church. I was quoting scripture," Bush responded indignantly and added, "If you don't believe in the word of the Lord, that's your problem."

"But isn't this a question of separation of church and state? When America's founding fathers were creating the Declaration of Independence in 1776, Thomas Jefferson wrote the first draft. He originally wrote, 'We hold these truths to be *sacred*, that all men are created equal.' After completing his first draft, Jefferson gave it to his friend Benjamin Franklin and asked for comments. Franklin rewrote the sentence to read, 'We hold these truths to be *self-evident*, that all men are created equal.' Benjamin Franklin was urging the founding fathers to create a nation in which democracy comes from reason, not religion—to make America's values the common sense of well-meaning people, not ordained by God."

"I've had about all his bullshit I can take," Bush said, looking over at his attorney. "Do I have to take any more of this from him?" Without waiting for an answer and much to the surprise of everyone in the courtroom, Bush stood up and headed toward the door.

White protested. "The prosecution has made a mockery of this case. It's disrespectful and abusive to President Bush, and disgusting and demeaning to all involved." With that, the defense attorneys quickly gathered their papers and followed Bush toward the exit.

Judge Harrison Hurst-Brown rapped his gavel. "Order in the Court. *Order in the Court.*"

Bush was blocked at the door by two ICC security guards, and other guards contained his defense team. It created a standoff of sorts: George Bush and his defense team versus the ICC guards.

"Mr. Bush," Hurst-Brown admonished, "you and your defense team need to go back to your respective seats and sit down. The Court will deal with this matter, but you need to sit down first before anything else can happen."

Bush and his defense team exchanged looks and, presumably figuring they couldn't push past the ICC guards and out the door, returned to their seats.

Once they were seated, Hurst-Brown turned to McBride. "Mr. McBride, do you have any further questions?"

"Yes, Your Honor, we do."

"Then you may continue."

"Thank you, Your Honor." McBride turned to Bush and continued his barrage. "Nine months into your war, no WMD had been found, Baghdad had fallen, and Saddam was captured. Did you ever consider stopping your war at that time?"

Bush seemed agitated and defensive. "Our goal was not just to get Saddam Hussein. Our goal was to bring freedom and democracy to Iraq, as I said before."

McBride shot back, "The people of Iraq didn't want or need your democracy. Since the beginning of recorded history, countries around the world have had various forms of governments: fascism, totalitarianism, communism, dictatorships. The peoples of a country should be free to follow whatever form of government they so choose. Some countries do not want and cannot support a democracy, whether the United States likes it or not. The Vietnam War, like your war, was a terrible war fought at a monumental cost of lives and money. And yet Vietnam never was going to be anything else but a communist country. The United States should have no say in how other sovereign countries wish to rule themselves. How would you like it if Russia or China invaded the United States and tried to dictate its form of government? Can't you see the problem here?"

Bush's answer dripped with disdain. "That's an absurd question, McBride, and you know it."

McBride didn't take the bait and moved on: "Your war converted an Iraq that was free of terrorists at that time into a safe haven for new militant extremist groups to form and grow. And as if all that isn't bad enough, your war angered and alienated the entire civilized world."

Bush began to fight back. "The nature of history is that people will only understand the consequences of actions we took in the future. But inaction would have consequences as well. Imagine what the world would be today with Saddam Hussein still ruling Iraq. He would be threatening his neighbors, sponsoring terror cells, and piling bodies into mass graves. The rising price of oil would have yielded him great wealth. And the American people would be much less secure. Instead, as a result of our actions, one of America's most dangerous enemies stopped threatening us forever. Hostile nations around the world saw clearly the cost of supporting terror and pursuing WMD. Twenty-five million Iraqis went from living under a dictatorship of fear to seeing the prospect of a peaceful, functioning democracy."

"George Bush, not surprisingly, you and I have different views of what military strength should be about. I definitely think America should have a strong military to protect and defend its people and their allies, not to attack and conquer, as America tried to do in Vietnam and Iraq."

"We weren't trying to *conquer* anybody," Bush protested. "We were trying to create a democracy where people could vote for their leaders and not live under the oppression of a ruthless and heartless tyrant. You have this wild-eyed compulsion to rewrite history."

Ignoring the insult, McBride pushed forward. "Early on in the war, you banned the American press from showing caskets of dead American soldiers when they returned home and from publicizing the growing number of American soldiers killed in your war. Why did you do that?"

Bush didn't answer.

McBride continued, "Was it because you didn't want the American people to realize you were exploiting their patriotism by putting their sons and daughters in harm's way for no good reason? Or was it because if they knew the truth about your war, there would have been anarchy in the streets, as there was during the Vietnam War? Huge public protests would likely have occurred all across the nation, and ultimately the American people would have demanded a stop to your war. And then, just maybe, you would've been impeached."

Bush looked over at White, apparently expecting him to object. Before he could, McBride added, "Yes, impeached. Then after you were disgracefully removed from office, you could've been tried in an American court for murder, like you are finally being tried in this Court."

White interjected again, "Objection! Baiting the witness."

"Objection sustained."

Bush answered anyway. "Presidents Roosevelt, Truman, Johnson, Nixon, Clinton, and my father waged wars and were not impeached. And they certainly didn't get tried."

McBride countered aggressively, "But why should American presidents get away with mass murder and other crimes if they wage a war against another country on the other side of the world that is not legally justifiable under international law?"

"You've got to get real, McBride. In the real world, those charged with governing sovereign nations have to make unimaginably tough judgments—real-time, live, immensely complicated judgments about war and peace. And they do so with the best interest of their people at heart."

"Okay. Let's talk about *the best interest* of your people. We know only too well the number of lives lost in your war. Less important but equally notable is the monetary cost of your war: four trillion dollars and counting . . . I say 'and counting' because, tragically, modern warfare kills fewer human beings and wounds more than in the past. It does so because body armor is more protective and medics are better equipped to save lives. Trillions of dollars have been spent and continue to be spent on the care and rehabilitation of brave American soldiers wounded physically and/or mentally in your war. If you want to talk about the 'best interest' of your people, think about all the good the money spent on war could do to fight poverty, illiteracy, hunger, climate change—and the list goes on."

Bush snapped back, "None of that would matter if America couldn't first defend herself against her enemies."

"George, try to see this for what it is. After 9/11 there was a tremendous outpouring of concern and sympathy from around the world for America. America's forefathers had built a country that represented hope and promise, freedom and opportunity, charity and compassion. If you would've taken out Osama bin Laden and neutered al Qaeda, everything would've been okay. But your war with Iraq ruptured and reversed the world's opinion of the United States."

Bush shook his head slowly. "You're trying to portray me as a vicious and evil man. I am not." He paused to collect himself. Everyone in the courtroom, public gallery, and around the world waited anxiously to hear what former president Bush would say next. Finally, with a hint of sadness, he continued, "The Iraq War was emotional for me. I prayed for the strength to do the Lord's will. I'm not trying to justify war based on God, but I prayed that I would be a good messenger of his will. I prayed for forgiveness."

Michael responded with a rare hint of compassion, "Once, when you took part in a presidential debate in St. Louis, a lady asked you to comment on the mistakes you made. Remember what you said?"

"When they asked about mistakes, they were trying to say, 'Did you make a mistake going into Iraq?' The answer is absolutely not. It was the right decision. I'm fully prepared to accept any mistakes that history judges to my administration, because the president makes the decisions. The president has to take the responsibility."

"Yes. Finally something we agree on. 'The president makes the decisions. The president has to take the responsibility.'" McBride turned to the judges. "No further questions at this time, Your Honors. The prosecution rests."

CHAPTER SEVENTEEN

A Winter's Nightmare

Each night, when I go to sleep, I die.
And the next morning, when I awake, I am reborn.
—Mahatma Gandhi

Winter in The Hague. There was seemingly no relief from the continuous long, cold, wet slog of dismal winter weather. Sunup was at eight thirty and daytime lasted eight hours. Each twenty-four hours was one-third day and two-thirds night. No doubt following the grueling prosecution questioning of former president Bush yesterday, all the participants in the case had a fitful night's sleep, with the possible exception of the judges.

George Bush's schedule complied with strict regulations mandated for all prisoners. Up at six thirty (at which time he would say his morning prayers), breakfast at seven, exercise, shave, shower, and dress (today, white button-down shirt, blue sweater, gray slacks). At eight thirty sharp, he was placed in an armored vehicle that pulled away under heavy protection. Once the military caravan turned right out of the compound, the ICC building two and a half kilometers down a perfectly straight road could be seen in the distance.

By nine a.m., everyone had assembled in his or her usual place, and the Court's day was beginning. Hurst-Brown addressed Bush's lead defense counsel. "Good morning, Mr. White. Would defense like to redirect questioning of this witness?"

"Yes, Your Honor, we most certainly would."

"Then you may proceed."

"Thank you, Your Honor." White stood and moved closer to his friend. "In the end, Mr. President, as we all know, war is tragic. A head of state has a seemingly endless number of tough decisions to make. He or she must do what in their heart they believe is right for the protection of their people and preservation of the common good. As you look back now, what thoughts do you have about that war?"

Bush seemed weary but he spoke clearly and carefully. "Over the years, I've spent a great deal of time thinking about what went wrong in Iraq. I have concluded that we made two errors. The first is that we did not respond more quickly or aggressively when the security situation started to deteriorate after Saddam's regime fell. In the ten months following the invasion, we cut troop levels from one hundred and ninety-two thousand to one hundred and nine thousand. That was a mistake. The second was the intelligence failure regarding Iraq's WMD. I believed that the intelligence on Iraq's WMD was solid. If Saddam didn't have WMD, why wouldn't he just prove it to the inspectors? He obviously never thought the United States would follow through on its promises to disarm him by force. If America is going to continue to be the leader of the free world, it must stand up to its obligations, as difficult and controversial and messy as they may be."

White continued, "Mr. Bush, isn't it true that the entire executive branch of the United States government, including Vice President Dick Cheney, Secretary of Defense Don Rumsfeld,

Secretary of State Colin Powell, National Security Advisor Condoleezza Rice, and others aggressively petitioned the US Congress to sanction the Iraq War?"

"Yes."

"And did you understand that the majority vote of the US Senate, including 'yea' votes from then senators Hillary Clinton and John Kerry, and the majority of the House of Representatives, provided clear and irrefutable approval of the Iraq War?"

"Yes."

"And such approval was near unanimously supported by the American people?"

"Yes."

"And following the overwhelming support of the United States Congress and the American people, the United Nations passed Resolution 1441, which demanded that Iraq comply with long-standing UN mandates or there would be 'serious consequences'?"

"Yes."

"And did you and others in your administration take 'serious consequences' to mean 'war' if necessary?"

"Yes."

"So in the months and weeks leading up to the Iraq War, you understood that you had the consent and approval of the US Congress, the American people, and the United Nations to wage war on Iraq and its ruthless dictator, Saddam Hussein?"

"Yes."

"And you were simply doing what was constitutionally required of you as the president of the United States?"

"Yes."

Believing he had successfully executed an important question-and-answer session with his client, White turned and said simply to the judges, "Thank you, Your Honors. May the strict application of the law be your guide. No further questions."

McBride seized the moment. "Your Honors, the prosecution requests permission to recross."

"Permission granted."

"Thank you. Your Honors, first let's set the record straight. The US Congress and UN Security Council authorizations do not provide legal defense against the prosecution of George Bush for war crimes. Congress only provided the authorization for Mr. Bush to 'protect and defend' America—not fight a war on the other side of the world against an enemy he did not have. And UN Resolution 1441 was only a relisting of complaints regarding Iraq's lack of compliance with past mandates, and did not specifically authorize the use of force. George Bush, and his friend Tony Blair for that matter, had no legal authority to wage their war against Iraq, and thus it is in breach of international law."

McBride turned to address the former president, who looked ten years older than he had when he arrived in The Hague three months earlier. "George Bush, your father was smart enough to leave Saddam alive and in power. You were not. Your selfish and disastrous war disrupted and disrespected the Muslim people and their religion. And now the rest of the world, including Christians, Jews, atheists, and others, are paying the price. Nobody won in your war, Mr. Bush. Everybody on all sides lost. Do you have anything else to say?"

Not only was everyone in the courtroom focused on him, but so also were those in the public gallery (including Laura), thousands outside watching the huge video monitors, and millions more in public areas of cities large and small around the world. The total viewership during this phase of the trial was estimated to be one billion people, approximately 14 percent of the world's population.

Finally, Bush looked McBride directly in the eye and answered, "No. Nothing I haven't already said."

"Okay. I have one last thing to ask. After the war your ally Tony Blair admitted he was wrong and apologized. There is something noble about a man who is brave enough to admit he was wrong, regardless of how painful it might be. Here's your chance—would you like to make an apology?"

After considering the question for a long moment, Bush answered. "No apology necessary. After the attacks of 9/11, I did what needed to be done to protect and defend the American people and to rebuild my nation's trust in its government. I made America a safer place. That's what I was charged to do, and that's what I did. I make no apologies for it. I am sorry for the loss of life on both sides, but, as history has proven, there is a great price to pay for freedom. I have a clear conscience about what I did. I am an American citizen first, and a citizen of the world second. Whatever this Court decides will never change my love for, and allegiance to, the United States of America."

McBride refused to leave it at that. "George, every human being is a citizen of the world, whether they like it or not. Just as you are a citizen of Texas, you are a citizen of the United States. Just as you are a citizen of the United States, you are a citizen of the world. And if you commit crimes of international consequence, you will be held accountable by the International Criminal Court, like everybody else in the world."

McBride stared at Bush who stared back and said nothing.

Finally, McBride turned to the judges. "No further questions, Your Honors."

Hurst-Brown gaveled and announced the case would be in recess until further notice. The clerk announced, "All rise." All did. The ICC judges stood and quickly made their exit.

CHAPTER EIGHTEEN

The Tale of Two Trials

*The wrongs which we seek to condemn and punish have
been so calculated, so malignant, and so devastating, that
civilization cannot tolerate their being ignored, because it
cannot survive their being repeated.*
—*Robert H. Jackson*

In truth, the Iraq War wasn't much of a fight. Within weeks,
Baghdad had fallen and for all intents and purposes the war was
over. The Iraq that was Iraq before the war was vanquished. Not
only did that war eventually kill nearly a million Iraqis; two million more were displaced from their homes. The newly formed
Iraqi government was never considered anything more than a
puppet regime of the United States, and over time it began to
unravel. George Bush's war destroyed the country of Iraq, at least
for the foreseeable future.

Following the war, most reputable Iraqis sought to perpet-
uate the Muslim way of life, find their own identity absent a
ruthless dictator or foreign invaders, and hold accountable those
who were responsible for the war. It was this mind-set that led
a group of patriotic Iraqis to petition the ICC to bring George
Bush to trial for war crimes.

With the ravages of his war still much in evidence, it was understandable that George Bush's trial received extensive coverage in Iraq. One of the web-based news agencies covering the trial was Aswat al-Iraq, which translates to "voices of Iraq." Aswat's writer, Nassim Bishara, who had studied history and law in both France and the United States, wrote the following essay after the conclusion of Bush's testimony: "It is evident that George W. Bush is being tried at the ICC under the well-established guidelines of international criminal law and has had the benefit of the defense counsel of his own choosing. In contrast to Bush's trial, let's look at the trial of Saddam Hussein.

"In December 2003, nine months into the war, US soldiers captured Hussein near his hometown of Tikrit. Most people who advocated for the protection of fundamental human rights and the just application of international law assumed an international criminal tribunal would try President Hussein. After all, such had been the case for other accused leaders such as Milošević, Karadzic, and Kony.

"But no such thing happened.

"After being held captive for a year and a half, Hussein was brought to trial in what was called the 'Iraqi High Tribunal' and charged with the killing of one hundred and forty-eight Shiite Iraqis in retaliation for an assassination attempt on his life in 1982. He was not charged for any crimes against America or other countries in the coalition.

"Before the trial, Hussein's defense team requested a delay in the proceedings, insisting they had not been given all the evidentiary materials that had been secured by the prosecution, and did not have sufficient time to evaluate the evidence they had been given. The request was denied.

"In his first trial appearance, Hussein vigorously rejected the tribunal's legitimacy and its independence from America's control, stating, 'I do not respond to this so-called court, and I retain my constitutional rights as the president of Iraq. Neither do I recognize the government that has designated and authorized you.'

"On 5 November 2006, Hussein was found guilty and sentenced to death by hanging.

"On 30 December 2006, at an Iraqi army base in Baghdad known as Camp Justice, Saddam Hussein, without having been provided the due process of law which is mandated for all human beings regardless of the severity of crime or crimes in question, was hung."

Nassim Bishara's final paragraph read: "There was much worldwide comment about the reaction to Hussein's death. In the United States, President George Bush stated, 'Saddam Hussein's trial is a milestone in the Iraqi people's efforts to replace the rule of a tyrant with the rule of law.' In Rome at the Vatican, Cardinal Martino said, 'For me, punishing a crime with another crime, which is what killing for vindication is, means that we are still at the point of demanding an eye for an eye, a tooth for a tooth.'"

CHAPTER NINETEEN

Final Arguments

War against a foreign country only happens when the
moneyed classes think they are going to profit from it.
—George Orwell

One of the things fans find so appealing about sporting competitions is that usually no one knows how an event will end. One team seems to have the upper hand, then the opposing team gains momentum, and back and forth it goes until finally there is a winner. Knowledgeable observers of the Bush trial admitted that, while each side had clear victories along the way, the outcome was impossible to predict.

There were reports that bookies in the UK offered a betting line with odds of fifty-five to forty-five on a verdict of Bush's innocence over guilt. Putting aside such frivolity, much was at stake, and this game had come down to the final moments. Prosecution versus defense. Guilt versus innocence. War versus peace. Who and what would prevail? There would be no ties in this game.

At nine o'clock the morning following the final day of Bush's testimony, a packed courtroom watched in silence as the three judges marched solemnly to their seats. What was at stake was abundantly clear. A guilty verdict would mean a former president of the United States could spend the rest of his life in prison, while a verdict of innocent would send George Bush home and leave open the possibility of more questionable wars in the future.

Judge Hurst-Brown gaveled the day to begin and called upon the prosecuting attorneys to make their final argument.

Following a year of pretrial research and investigation, and three months of trial, Michael McBride stood to make the prosecution's final argument—an argument no doubt intended to stick the proverbial dagger into George Bush's heart.

While fatigued beyond description from sleepless nights and more pressure than most humans could bear without buckling, McBride stood erect as he addressed the Court in a clear and solemn voice. "Your Honors, the implications of this trial are of great historical importance. No one can deny the gravity of bringing a former American president to the International Criminal Court to stand trial for war crimes. But in finality, you three judges are called upon to do what you do every day: apply the law as it relates to the conduct of humankind.

"A bedrock principle of justice holds that every man is equal before the law—pauper or president, president or pauper. As this Court has noted, no one, including leaders of superpowers, has impunity for acts he or she undertook while in office, and war crimes carry no statute of limitations. George Bush cannot hide from his crimes, and he cannot hide from this Court. He is liable for his crimes just like anybody else, and remains so until the day he dies.

"Both documentary evidence and witness testimony have proven that the man seated before you today, George Bush, is guilty of war crimes. During testimony he admitted as much himself. He revealed his intent to pursue a war that was illegal under international law and in blatant disregard for the conse-quences he knew would result from his war.

"Article 25(3) of the Rome Statute states, 'A person shall be criminally responsible and liable for punishment for a crime within the jurisdiction of the Court if that person: a) commits such a crime, whether as an individual, jointly with another or through another person, regardless of whether that other person is criminally responsible; b) orders, solicits or induces the com-mission of such a crime which in fact occurs or is attempted; c) for the purpose of facilitating the commission of such a crime, aids, abets or otherwise assists in its commission or its attempted commission, including providing the means for its commis-sion; d) in any other way contributes to the commission or the attempted commission of such a crime by a group of persons acting with a common purpose.'"

McBride turned to the judges and pled with all his heart. "Your Honors, the prosecution has proven beyond any reasonable doubt that George Bush is guilty of each and every one of these acts . . . a, b, c, and d as stated above . . . and must be found guilty.

"As president of the United States, not only was George Bush the chief executive officer, but also the constitutionally mandated commander in chief. As such, he was in charge of all armed forces at the disposal of the US government.

"Under the 'command responsibility doctrine,' as the chain of command in the United States ends with the president, the president must be—and is—the person most responsible for the commission of crimes. Through this well-established legal con-cept, the perpetrator need not have pulled the trigger to commit the crime. Courts have long held that a commander who orders his subordinates to act unlawfully bears full responsibility for the actions that follow from his orders.

"Additionally, we urge the Court to find George Bush guilty of crimes under the legal doctrine known as 'joint criminal enterprise.' In a war such as the Iraq War, soldiers are considered merely innocents doing their duty as ordered by their commander. The commander is criminally liable—as he had the duty to know and identify civilian versus combatant targets in the field of battle.

"Next, with respect to 'derivative liability' we urge you to find the accused guilty of war crimes under Article (25)(3)(c), which includes the concept of 'aiding and abetting.' Under this form of liability, George Bush aided and abetted by virtue of the fact he secured congressional approval and ordered the US military into action, which inexorably led to the commission of these crimes. Your Honors, respectfully I remind the Court that aiding and abetting carries the same penalty as if one committed the crime or crimes personally.

"George Bush ordered the invasion of Iraq in blatant disregard of international law and in reckless disdain for the terrible consequences that would certainly follow. He engaged an army that was underprepared to conduct postwar humanitarian operations and untrained in the proper handling of prisoners of war. Tragically, he empowered a military force with the most technologically advanced weaponry available to exact the maximum amount of death and destruction on an imagined enemy."

McBride paused to give the judges time to consider his assertions, and then continued. "Your Honors, the weight of this decision is great. With four thousand eight hundred and forty-five coalition soldiers and as many as six hundred and fifty thousand Iraqi citizens dead as a result of George Bush's war, the implications of your decision will impact countless victims and their survivors. No doubt your decision will set important legal precedent for the future. That weight is no greater than what should be resting on the conscience of George Bush. However, as he appears to be unwavering in his certainty about being right, that is sadly not the case."

McBride's voice grew in volume and emotional intensity. "After the attacks of September 11, 2001, the great majority of the world's population would have understood America hunting down and bringing to justice those who carried out the attacks: al Qaeda and Osama bin Laden. But for whatever incomprehensible reason, George Bush did not do that.

"Tragically, we all know the results of his war. Not only were al Qaeda and the Taliban not destroyed; they got stronger. Radical Muslims in the Middle East banded together to protect their religious rights and principles. The Islamic State took form. They struck back—a faceless enemy without a geographical home—recruiting and training disenfranchised youths over the Internet to fight an unholy jihad. And all of it can be traced back to George Bush's war.

"In truth, America would have been better off if Mr. Bush had *befriended* Saddam Hussein—like President Reagan did in the Iran-Iraq War—rather than destroying him, because he may well have stopped the creation of ISIS before it started."

McBride couldn't tell if the judges were with him or not. So he continued his plea with even more passion. "Your Honors, the evidence is clear. Common sense makes it even more obvious. George Bush waged an illogical, illegal, and unnecessary war. Now you, the judges of the International Criminal Court, must determine his fate.

"In so doing, you may well be determining the destiny of humankind. Finding him innocent will doom our children and our children's children to a world of hate, fear, aggression, and more wars. Finding him guilty will send a clear message to all heads of state that they can no longer wage unnecessary and illegal wars against sovereign nations with impunity. In just this way, you may turn the tide of humanity away from its seemingly irresistible urge to fight military battles.

"Here and now, this Court represents the hopes and dreams of all peace-loving peoples of the world. What will it be: Love or hate? Peace or war? Survival or destruction? Your Honors, you must have the courage to discharge your duties under the oath you took when accepting your appointment as a judge in this Court to uphold the law. Simply put, the destiny of humankind could be at stake."

The judges sat motionless. McBride paused for a moment and then went for the big finish. "In the name of justice—out of respect for the dignity of all humankind—in pursuit of swift and sure application of international law—in validation of what the International Criminal Court was intended to be—and in the precious quest for peace on earth, we ask you, the esteemed judges who have so effectively presided over this case . . . *No*, the peoples of the world *plead with you* to find George Bush guilty of one or more of the war crimes of which he is accused, and of which he is so clearly guilty. Thank you, Your Honors. Thank you. The prosecution rests."

"Thank you, Mr. McBride," Hurst-Brown announced with all due ceremony. "Defense may proceed with final arguments."

Ed White glanced at his friend who sat alone and vulnerable in the accused box. Bush smiled a half-hearted smile. White winked back, stood, cleared his throat, and began. "Thank you, Your Honor. In World War II, free nations came together to fight the ideologies of fascism and imperialism—Adolf Hitler in Germany and Hideki Tojo in Japan—and freedom prevailed. Today, both Germany and Japan are vibrant democracies and much-trusted members of the international community of sovereign nations.

"Who is to say the young democracy that is trying to survive in Iraq will not in time be the very thing that ultimately transitions Iraq from an isolated rogue nation to a thriving country recognized as a member in good standing by friendly countries around the globe?

"The results of war are often not understood until years after the final shots are fired. The prosecution's contention is that what happened in Iraq was an international armed conflict. It was not. It was a strategic mission by the United States and its allies to specifically remove a known terrorist from power. No one could dispute that Saddam Hussein had been a threat to the United States and had waged various forms of warfare against her allies including Israel and Kuwait. Given Saddam Hussein's violent temper and aggressive conduct over decades, and given the availability of more sophisticated and mobile weaponry—in the chaos following the 9/11 attacks—he clearly posed an immediate and direct threat to the United States.

"Moreover, strictly speaking in legal terms, Mr. Bush could not be guilty of crimes during the Iraq War for the simple reason that Congress passed a joint resolution authorizing him to use the armed forces of the United States as he determined to be necessary in order to defend America. I emphasize *as he determined to be necessary*—not how the prosecution or, with all due respect, even the judges here at the ICC determine. To underscore the enthusiasm that Congress had for authorizing the Iraq War, after Mr. Bush's speech the assemblage rose up in unison and gave him a two-minute standing ovation.

"Furthermore, the United Nations Security Council had unanimously passed a joint resolution admonishing Iraq for past noncompliance with regard to weapons inspections and mandated new inspections. How can anyone treat Mr. Bush like a criminal for doing the very thing he was elected to do by the American people, and authorized to do by both the United States Congress and the United Nations?"

White turned toward the judges to deliver what he believed would be a knockout blow. "Your Honors, at this time I would like to introduce the attorney general of the United States, and with the permission of the Court, yield the floor to him so he can deliver a message from the president."

The entire courtroom reacted with surprise as US attorney general Thomas K. Harding, dressed in a conservative dark blue suit and exuding an air of impervious confidence, entered the courtroom and headed toward the defense table.

The ICC judges conferred.

The prosecuting attorneys debated what, if anything, they could do.

The defense attorneys welcomed their comrade.

The hubbub in the courtroom was silenced when Hurst-Brown rapped his gavel and stated, "The Court recognizes Attorney General Harding and welcomes him. Sir, would you please read the swearing-in document."

Shadid stood to protest. "Objection, Your Honors. This highly irregular stunt the defense is attempting, and you are condoning, violates well-established legal doctrines and protocol. The prosecution requests a recess in order to properly frame a response, and to prepare for cross-examination should it be needed."

Hurst-Brown responded immediately. "Thank you, Ms. Shadid. The prosecution's objection is noted but denied. The defense has only asked permission for the attorney general to submit a request to the Court. No interactive questions will be asked and no testimony given. Objection overruled."

Reluctantly, Shadid sat.

Harding read the swearing-in document and then looked up and confidently smiled at the judges. Hurst-Brown said, "Thank you, sir. You may proceed."

"Thank you, Your Honor. Good day and greetings to all assembled. First, I would like to apologize to the Court for my rather abrupt and irregular entrance. The increasing gravity of these proceedings has caught the attention of the president of the United States, who in turn requested I take immediate and appropriate action. I appear before you as an official emissary of both the president of the United States and the US Department of Justice.

"We consider the abduction of former president George W. Bush by the ICC to be in blatant violation of international laws and hold all those who participated in these uncalled-for and illegal acts responsible in both the jurisdictions of the ICC and criminal courts in the United States. Perforce, we categorically reject the ICC's contention that it had the necessary legal authority to transfer former president Bush here to The Hague and force him to stand trial in this Court. It is worth noting that the United States, as a member of the United Nations and specifically a permanent member of the Security Council, was party to the ratification of the ICC, and from the beginning has worked to support many of its organizational and procedural needs.

"However, along with registering the considerable objection of the American people for the illegal and disrespectful treatment of a former president, I come with a proposal.

"As you must know, one of the original tenets of international law is the important principle of admissibility, as defined by the 'complementarity rule.' For those unaware, Article 17 of the Rome Statute provides that the ICC shall consider a case admissible only when the home state of the alleged perpetrator—in this case the United States of America—is 'unwilling or unable to genuinely carry out the investigation.' This important doctrine of the ICC charter is meant to protect against and specifically disallow unnecessary prosecution, such as this.

"Speaking on behalf of the president of the United States and the US Justice Department, I hereby inform the ICC that the United States *invokes this complementarity rule* and requests Mr. Bush's immediate release so that he can be returned to his home country to be tried for the alleged offenses of which he is accused by this chamber."

Pandemonium broke out both inside and outside the Court.

Hurst-Brown had to repeatedly pound his gavel and call for order. Eventually the courtroom fell silent and Harding calmly and politely continued, "We do not wish to disrupt or invalidate the ICC. Nor do we wish to bring military action against the ICC. We simply request that the ICC immediately discharge Mr. Bush and turn him over to the custody of the United States, in which case he will be transported back to the United States to stand trial. We have a fleet of US military jets standing by, and I will personally escort him home."

McBride stood to interrupt. "Your Honors, prosecution requests the opportunity to respond."

Hurst-Brown replied, "First, we ask the attorney general if he has anything else to say."

"No, sir. Our request is simple and we expect the ICC to look upon it favorably."

Hurst-Brown was unsatisfied. "Is it the intention of the United States to put Mr. Bush on trial in the near future?"

Harding sidestepped the question. "Meaning?"

"As soon as practical."

"How would you define 'as soon as practical,' sir?"

Knowing that if he wanted to get the answer he needed, he had to give the judges an answer they would accept, the attorney general replied, "The United States will endeavor to commence the trial within twelve months of Mr. Bush's release from the ICC."

"*Endeavor* to commence, or *commit* to commence?"

If this were a chess game, the attorney general would have been put in check. He considered the implications of his answer carefully before speaking. "The United States will commit to commence the trial within twelve months of Mr. Bush's release."

"Thank you, Mr. Harding." Hurst-Brown then turned to McBride and Shadid. "Does the prosecution wish to address the Court on this matter?"

"Yes, Your Honor, we do," McBride said, standing.

"Please proceed."

McBride began. "Respectfully, Your Honors, this request by the United States cannot and must not be granted. The Iraq War was over in December of 2011 and under any fair assessment, the United States has had more than enough time to have brought charges against George Bush.

"Moreover, Article 17 of the Rome Statute provides that when the home state has decided 'not to prosecute the person concerned,' or 'there has been an *unjustified delay* in the proceedings' demonstrating the 'unwillingness or inability of the state genuinely to prosecute,' the jurisdiction of the case transfers to the ICC. The United States has had more than enough time to prosecute this case and must be deemed to have defaulted on its obligation. The people of Iraq, the people of the United States, indeed all the peoples of the world, deserve to have this case adjudicated upon, and a decision rendered, by the most universally accepted of all courts, the International Criminal Court. And, respectfully, a decision must be reached immediately."

Hoping he had not overstepped his bounds, McBride took a more measured approach. "Your Honors, this is nothing but international grandstanding by the United States meant to mock and demean this Court of international justice, something the United States is good at. The ICC must see this ploy for what it is, and in the name of international justice, deny this unwelcome and impertinent request here and now."

"Thank you Mr. McBride, your concerns are duly noted," Hurst-Brown stated before rapping his gavel and proclaiming, "This Court is adjourned until such time as we the judges of the ICC can reflect upon this unprecedented request from the United States and render judgment."

With that, Hurst-Brown rapped his gavel a final time, bringing to an end a notably important and precedent-setting day in the life of the International Criminal Court.

CHAPTER TWENTY

Can There Be Justice?

If there's not justice for the high and mighty like justice for the common man, then there is no justice.

—Anonymous

The events in The Hague set off an international explosion of press reports that ricocheted around the world. The world's experts on international law had provided months of commentary on what might or might not happen in the case, but none had imagined this.

In the United States, while legal experts, politicians, public employees, college law students, military brass, and news junkies debated the case nonstop, other Americans were content to go about their lives and catch updates on the evening news.

In both the United States and the UK, as the public was divided nearly equally in their opinions about the case, the reporting needed to be balanced so as to not overly advocate for one side or the other and thus anger half the audience.

In her segment on the BBC following the US attorney general's appearance at The Hague, Elizabeth Reynolds asked international legal scholar Professor Yuji Wakahisa to provide some legal perspective, which he did. "For those of you who are not legal junkies, the 'complementarity rule' in international law simply means that all states, including those that are not members of the ICC, have a duty to either prosecute suspected perpetrators of international crimes or extradite them to the ICC for trial.

"The only way the ICC can hear a case is if that state is 'unable or unwilling to genuinely prosecute' the matter in question. The principle here is that national governments must be allowed to prosecute first, if they so choose. If they cannot or do not, then the ICC comes in as a backup."

Reynolds pressed the professor for clarification. "But here, the United States is invoking the complementarity rule, even though the Iraq War ended more than a decade ago. In international law, is there a statute of limitations? How long can a state procrastinate?"

"Yes, this sequence of events is highly unusual. The complementarity principle is silent on the question of time. This case may well provide the legal precedent necessary for such matters in the future. The ICC judges would be within their rights, under strictly interpreted provisions of the Rome Statute, to deny this request. But it is a judgment call. They may elect to invoke the 'spirit' of the Rome Statute, which clearly allows for states to have the first crack at a case, irrespective of time, and thus allow the Americans to prosecute as they are pledging to do now."

"What would that do to the credibility of the ICC, Professor?"

"From the perspective of the international community, the ICC has demonstrated with this case that it means business. The fact that it brought the case to trial in the first place is a huge victory, not only for its credibility but also for its legitimacy. Early on in the case the judges countered very difficult legal challenges from defense attorney Edward White and succeeded nobly in defending the ICC's right to hear the case. Indeed, if the ICC does decide to step aside in favor of the complementarity rule, and let the United States go ahead and prosecute, it might even be applauded for its flexibility and deference to the sovereignty of individual states, thereby refuting many of the last remaining arguments against the ICC, especially from Republicans in the US Senate."

"What might happen if the ICC denied this request of the United States?"

"Well, presumably the case would continue at the ICC until a verdict was rendered. But the big question then would be, if George Bush *is* found guilty, how would the American people respond and what would the American government do, if anything?"

"And what would happen if the United States does not commence the trial in a year as they pledged to the Court they would do?"

"All bets would be off the table and you could look for George Bush to be snatched again."

Reynolds concluded with a wry hint of intrigue. "High drama indeed at the International Criminal Court. Stay tuned for continuing coverage."

The following morning all the principal dramatis personae had assembled in the courtroom, including the US attorney general. Bush wore his most presidential blue suit, white shirt, and red tie.

Presiding judge Hurst-Brown gaveled and announced the Court back in session. He came right to the point with breathtaking abruptness. "Regarding the unprecedented request registered on behalf of the president of the United States and the US

State Department, the Court has reached a decision—a unanimous decision, I might add."

McBride and Shadid glanced at each other. Years of study, work, and preparation would come down to the next few seconds.

Hurst-Brown continued, "The 'principle of complementarity' was an important concept in the initial formation of international criminal law. In fact, it was envisioned and drafted at the time by the greatest legal minds in the world. It was of unanimous consent that the state in which the perpetrator of a crime domiciled had the first rights of prosecution, deliberation, and decision with regard to guilt or innocence. In fact, the International Criminal Court would cease to fulfill its mandated purpose if it breeched this fundamental concept. While there are serious questions about the length of time it has taken the United States to exercise its right to first prosecution—its fundamental rights relative to the complementarity rule remain in force."

Rapping his gavel three times, Hurst-Brown took a deep breath and issued the much-anticipated ruling. "In the case of *The Prosecutor v. George W. Bush*, this Court yields to the request of the United States and agrees to release Mr. Bush into the custody of its officials with the understanding they will transport him back to the United States to stand trial within a period of twelve months from this date for crimes he is alleged to have committed in connection with the Iraq War."

Pandemonium erupted. Those in the public gallery and elsewhere who wanted Bush to be found guilty responded with loud and indignant outrage. Those in support of Bush's innocence were cheering and hugging one another with joy and relief.

Inside the courtroom, the defense was alternately hugging Bush and shaking the attorney general's hand.

The prosecution was equal parts outraged and crestfallen.

The ICC courtroom staff was dumbfounded.

The judges sat stone-faced.

McBride rose to his feet. "Your Honors, please! The prosecution pleads for the opportunity to respond."

Hurst-Brown pounded his gavel to regain order and be heard. "Permission granted."

With shocking intensity, McBride launched into his objections: "Your Honors, this Court has buckled under this highly irregular and ridiculously tardy pressure placed upon it by the United States. This attempted rupture of justice more than a decade after the crimes were committed *would not only set, but would ensure, the dangerous precedent* that other states will simply monitor the proceedings at the ICC, and if they're not comfortable with the likely outcome, they will *invoke the complementarity rule*—and the ICC will be forced by this precedent to yield. The inmates will be running the asylum. This will go down in history as a sad day in the life of the ICC specifically, and for international criminal law in general. I hope you understand the gravity of this, Your Honors, because you will have been responsible for it."

Hurst-Brown immediately, and without consulting his fellow judges, fired a return volley. "I caution you, Mr. McBride; you are moments away from being found in contempt and removed from this Court."

McBride held fire.

Hurst-Brown paused to make sure order had been restored and then continued, "Mr. McBride, the judges of the ICC do not need a lecture, nor do we need to be scolded."

McBride acquiesced. "Yes, Your Honor. Apologies."

Seemingly satisfied with McBride's modest gesture of conciliation, Hurst-Brown responded, "Apologies accepted. Now, would you like to continue?"

"Yes, Your Honor."

"Then do so."

McBride swung around to address the attorney general, George Bush, the defense team, and all others assembled in the courtroom. "For America to be the great nation it once was, it must take responsibility for the mistakes it makes. These mistakes certainly include those made by George Bush in connection with the Iraq War. George, you waged your war with a coalition of military forces. If you are not found guilty—which I hope to God you are—how about you personally assembling a coalition of humanitarian forces to fix the mess you most certainly created in Iraq and the Middle East?

"Instead of fighting unnecessary wars, we should be focusing our combined resources on solving problems that would elevate the human condition—problems such as hunger, illiteracy, poverty, illness, slavery, homelessness, child abuse, drug abuse, and so many others we could name. How about we stop beating each other up and turn our collective attention to the very things that can make the human condition better, smarter, healthier, more compassionate, tolerant, sane, safe, and, yes . . . loving?"

McBride paused to wonder if anybody cared about what he was saying and then soldiered on. "I plead that at the very minimum this case will send a message to all peoples of the world—especially our youth—that they should not and must not go blindly into war just because their government tells them to, especially when considering that it is less than 1 percent of the population—certain government officials, military brass, and the press—who take the entire nation to war. Every human being should have a say about the conduct of their own lives and the behavior of their country, whether it contradicts the wishes of their government or not."

An awkward silence pervaded the courtroom before McBride, torn asunder by emotions, fired his final shot. "The US government may have temporarily won this battle, but it has not won the war—the war that exists in the hearts and minds of the peoples of the world between injustice and justice, cruelty and compassion, war and peace, hate and love."

Then, in a shocking act of defiance and disrespect, McBride abruptly marched out of the courtroom.

People sat stunned and silent. Nobody knew quite what to say or do. Eventually, Shadid followed him out.

Judge Hurst-Brown rapped his gavel and said in a somber and somewhat weary voice, "*The Prosecutor v. George W. Bush* is closed, for the time being."

White moved to former president Bush and hugged him triumphantly, saying, "Let's go home, George."

Bush sighed. "Yeah. I've had about all the fun here I can stand."

There was not much joy among Bush and his defense team as they quickly packed their papers and headed for the exit. One could sense a tentative, awkward feeling of relief, more than accomplishment. They knew full well this game was not over.

Not far off the coast in the North Sea, the order was given to maneuver the USS *George H. W. Bush* to a southerly heading for immediate departure, destination unknown.

CHAPTER TWENTY-ONE

All Over but the Shouting

The care of human life and happiness,
and not their destruction, is the first and only
legitimate object of good government.
—Thomas Jefferson

There is something disappointing, if not infuriating, about a story that does not end. In theory, the United States had the moral obligation to live up to its pledge to put former president Bush on trial. No one can be sure of it, however, until it happens.

Some judicial scholars were critical of the prosecutors, McBride and Shadid, for not winning a case that so many thought needed to be won for no lesser reason than the safety and security of all humankind. In the end, the ICC got mostly high marks for bringing George Bush to trial and low marks for not rendering a final verdict.

There were many residual questions that only time would answer. Will the United States put George Bush on trial? Will it happen in the twelve months allotted? What will be the verdict? If Bush was to be found innocent in American courts, would the ICC be able to recapture him and bring him back to The Hague to finish what it started? If, in the future, other leaders of superpowers wage illegal wars, will the Bush trial have provided enough precedent and legitimacy for the ICC to bring the alleged perpetrators to stand trial for their crimes? If, in the future, leaders of superpowers are brought to trial at the ICC, will their home state simply monitor the case and, if a verdict of guilty seems inevitable, invoke the complementarity rule as was done by the United States in the Bush case? Will the ICC have secured its place as the legitimate international court that stands above all national courts, regardless of the implications of the case? Will the case of *The Prosecutor v. George W. Bush* have made the world a safer place, or not?

Even though Laura had brought him clothes, for his own reasons George Bush wanted to walk out of the detention center in the same clothes he wore when he walked in. As he finished putting on the golf clothes he wore at St. Andrews, he took one last look around the prison cell that had been his home for nearly four months and walked out.

It was Bush's wish not to "sneak out of town," as he put it, but rather to make a proper exit—the exit of a confident man who knew all along he had done no wrong. Waiting in the foyer of the detention center were Laura Bush, his three defense attorneys, six UN security guards, and a dozen armed US military personnel.

When Bush arrived in the foyer, he was greeted with a warm embrace from his wife, after which were handshakes and hugs from his defense team. Not much was said. They all knew only too well what had happened was not an ending, but rather only served to prompt questions of what was yet to come.

Mr. Bush took Mrs. Bush's hand and, with more relief than triumph, walked out of the detention center.

There was no order to the assembled crowd outside. Some waved placards that read, "We Love You President Bush," "Justice Is Served," and "God Loves You George." Other placards displayed the opposite sentiment: "George Bush, Murderer," "Hope You Burn in Hell," "Iraq's Blood Is on Your Hands." The yelling of the crowd mirrored the sentiments of the placards.

Standing side by side, some were yelling congratulations and well wishes to the former president and others were screaming their protests, hatred, and threats. During the brief walk Bush noticed a teenage girl in the crowd waving an American flag. He smiled, nodded his approval, and held up two fingers, flashing the "V" for "victory" sign, a gesture that thrilled some and angered others.

Other than making sure no one got too close to the Bushes, the escort team simply moved them through the crowd and into the helicopter. Wanting to avoid undue delay, the chopper pilot had done his preflight check and the blades were whirling. The helicopter lifted off and whisked George Bush away from the International Criminal Court and to a US military jet that would transport him back home to America.

As the chopper lifted, the crowd availed themselves of the moment to yell their final good-byes or invectives. When the aircraft disappeared in the distance, the people were left standing still and silent. Some wondered why others could be so ignorant as to not comprehend the horrible destruction of George Bush's war and the woeful miscarriage of justice that his escape from international justice represented. Others wondered why some people could have so much hatred in their hearts that they couldn't grant love and forgiveness. Still others concluded that justice was served and that there was no need for apologies, or forgiveness, from or for anybody.

Later that night a very curious thing occurred. Nobody could find Michael McBride.

Nadia and Michael had agreed to meet back in the prosecution offices to start packing up the mountain of evidence they had accumulated. But after Nadia had been working for more than an hour, she realized Michael was not coming. She tried his various phone numbers with no luck. She went to his house in a suburb near the ICC, but the lights were out and no one responded to knocks at the door.

The following morning Nadia called Michael's wife in London and, trying not to alarm her, simply inquired as to his whereabouts. Mrs. Stapleford-McBride said she had not heard from him in weeks and guessed he would eventually surface. This was how he dealt with defeat. Maybe *she* believes that, Nadia thought, but that wasn't the Michael McBride she knew.

At the end of her second day of searching, Nadia alerted administrators at the ICC, who in turn notified local police. Michael McBride, a highly respected and by now famous prosecuting attorney at the ICC, was placed on a missing persons list, first in Europe, then around the world, where he remains to this day.

Author's Notes

I would like to be completely transparent regarding material in this book that was written or spoken by others. In some ways, I was more an aggregator of content than a writer, and I would like to acknowledge the many sources used herein. Relying on the original authors for veracity, I have used material from the following books (listed alphabetically by author's last name):

Allawi, Ali A. *The Occupation of Iraq: Winning the War, Losing the Peace*. New Haven: Yale University Press, 2007.

Blair, Tony. *A Journey: My Political Life*. New York: Knopf, 2010.

Bush, George W. *Decision Points*. New York: Crown, 2010.

Bush, Laura. *Spoken from the Heart*. New York: Scribner, 2010.

Cheney, Richard B. *In My Time*. New York: Threshold Editions, 2011.

Clarke, Richard A. *Against All Enemies: Inside America's War on Terror*. New York: Free Press, 2004.

Franks, Tommy. *American Soldier*. New York: Regan Books, 2004.

Isikoff, Michael, and David Corn. *Hubris: The Inside Story of Spin, Scandal, and the Selling of the Iraq War*. New York: Crown, 2006.

Kukis, Mark. *Voices from Iraq: A People's History, 2003–2009*. New York: Columbia University Press, 2011.

Oborne, Peter. *Not the Chilcot Report*. London: Head of Zeus, 2016.

Rice, Condoleezza. *No Higher Honor: A Memoir of My Years in Washington*. New York: Crown, 2011.

Ricks, Thomas E. *Fiasco: The American Military Adventure in Iraq*. New York: Penguin, 2006.

Riverbend. *Baghdad Burning: Girl Blog from Iraq*. New York: The Feminist Press at CUNY, 2005.

Rumsfeld, Donald. *Known and Unknown: A Memoir*. New York: Sentinel, 2011.

Schabas, William A. *An Introduction to the International Criminal Court. 4th ed*. Cambridge: Cambridge University Press, 2011.

Woodward, Bob. *Plan of Attack: The Definitive Account of the Decision to Invade Iraq*. New York: Simon & Schuster, 2004.

Wright, Evan. *Generation Kill: Devil Dogs, Ice Man, Captain America, and the New Face of American War*. New York: Putnam, 2004.

Following is a list of the sources from which I have taken specific quotes. Some are not verbatim but rather edited and shaped to be dialogue rather than prose. The page number where each quote can be found is also included.

53 "fall into the hands of terrorists." George Bush, *Decision Points*.

65 "Nothing today justifies war." George Bush, *Decision Points*.

96 "I am female." Riverbend, *Baghdad Burning*.

97 "Who will read it?" Riverbend, *Baghdad Burning*.

97 "expect a lot of complaining . . ." Riverbend, *Baghdad Burning*.

97 "Today a child was killed . . ." Riverbend, *Baghdad Burning*.

98 "Sergio de Mello's death . . ." Riverbend, *Baghdad Burning*.

98 "don't let the name fool you." Riverbend, *Baghdad Burning*.

98 "Bush must be proud today . . ." Riverbend, *Baghdad Burning*.

99 "The article basically states . . ." Riverbend, *Baghdad Burning*.

99 "Events in the United States are not helping . . ." Riverbend, *Baghdad Burning*.

100 "war started during the early . . ." Riverbend, *Baghdad Burning*.

101 "the day the Iraqi puppets . . ." Riverbend, *Baghdad Burning*.

103 "Don't blame the Muslim religion." Riverbend, *Baghdad Burning*.

104 "When I hear 'anti-American' . . ." Riverbend, *Baghdad Burning*.

107 "Paul Wolfowitz . . . 'I just don't understand why' . . ." Clarke, *Against All Enemies*.

108 "had no real interest in the complicated . . ." Clarke, *Against All Enemies*.

109 "Nowhere on the list of things . . ." Clarke, *Against All Enemies*.

110 "now seen as a 'super-bully' . . ." Clarke, *Against All Enemies*.

110 "When the United States needs international . . ." Clarke, *Against All Enemies*.

110 "If it were not for the American invasion of Iraq . . . there would be no ISIS." Richard A. Clarke, in *Long Road to Hell: America in Iraq*, hosted by Fareed Zakaria, CNN, October 26, 2015, transcript, http://www.cnn.com/TRANSCRIPTS/1510/26/csr.01.html.

114 "American Light Armored Reconnaissance . . ." Wright, *Generation Kill*.

114 "Early the next morning . . ." Wright, *Generation Kill*.

116 "Coalition ground, naval, air, and Special Operations . . ." Franks, *American Soldier*.

116 "all key infrastructure improvements . . ." Franks, *American Soldier*.

119 "Thanks to the decisions America's leaders . . ." Franks, *American Soldier*.

119 "History will record that . . ." Franks, *American Soldier*.

119 "Today, thanks largely to . . ." Franks, *American Soldier*.

119 "I am frequently asked . . ." Franks, *American Soldier*.

120 "British philosopher Edmund Burke . . ." Franks, *American Soldier*.

124 "I was surprised . . ." Franks, *American Soldier*.

126 "Millions of men and women have worn . . ." Franks, *American Soldier*.

127 "I did not agree with every decision made . . ." Franks, *American Soldier*.

127 "I wish some things had been done differently . . ." Franks, *American Soldier*.

127 "I have said, and will continue to say . . ." Franks, *American Soldier*.

133 "it is easy to forget now . . ." Rice, *No Higher Honor*.

133 "clear that the immediate problem was the . . ." Rice, *No Higher Honor*.

134 "to produce a joint assessment known as the National . . ." Rice, *No Higher Honor*.

134 "If left unchecked . . ." George Bush, *Decision Points*.

135 "Saddam was a known supporter of terrorism." Rice, *No Higher Honor*.

135 "were down to two options if we wanted to . . ." Rice, *No Higher Honor*.

135 "the question of how to remove Saddam . . ." Rice, *No Higher Honor.*

135 "The Egyptians claimed . . ." Rice, *No Higher Honor.*

136 "the beginning of 2003, I was convinced . . ." Rice, *No Higher Honor.*

136 "Hussein was a cancer in the Middle East . . ." Rice, *No Higher Honor.*

137 "In light of this threat, limiting . . ." Rice, *No Higher Honor.*

139 "Tenet briefed us on the evidence of al Qaeda's . . ." Rice, *No Higher Honor.*

139 "prepare to go to war against al Qaeda . . ." Rice, *No Higher Honor.*

140 "revoked, bin Laden returned . . ." Rice, *No Higher Honor.*

140 "Paul Wolfowitz, who started talking about Iraq . . ." Rice, *No Higher Honor.*

140 "I remember thinking . . ." Rice, *No Higher Honor.*

140 "the president asked each member . . ." Rice, *No Higher Honor.*

141 "the president went before the American public . . ." Rice, *No Higher Honor.*

141 "US planes bombed the few installations . . ." Rice, *No Higher Honor.*

142 "It was well understood . . ." Rice, *No Higher Honor.*

142 "Those efforts were frustrating and largely . . ." Rice, *No Higher Honor.*

143 "the art, not the science of piecing . . ." Rice, *No Higher Honor.*

144 "The activities we detected do not add up . . ." Rice, *No Higher Honor.*

146 "The fact is, we invaded Iraq because . . ." Rice, *No Higher Honor.*

147 "in the end he comes to his own decision . . ." Rice, *No Higher Honor.*

158 "To ensure compliance, Saddam . . ." George Bush, *Decision Points.*

159 "We believed Saddam's weakness was . . ." George Bush, *Decision Points.*

159 "to rally a coalition of nations to make clear that Saddam's . . ." George Bush, *Decision Points.*

159 "Before 9/11, Saddam was a problem America might have . . ." George Bush, *Decision Points.*

159 "The stakes were too high to trust . . ." George Bush, *Decision Points*.

160 "a sworn enemy of the United States." George Bush, *Decision Points*.

160 "He'd fired at our aircraft, praised 9/11 . . ." George Bush, *Decision Points*.

160 "Saddam didn't just . . . he *used* them." George Bush, *Decision Points*.

160 "He deployed mustard gas and nerve agents . . ." George Bush, *Decision Points*.

161 "I'm with you, Mr. President." George Bush, *Decision Points*.

161 "Are UN Security Council resolutions to be honored . . ." George Bush, *Decision Points*.

161 "or will it be rendered irrelevant?" George Bush, *Decision Points*.

161 "The vote was unanimous . . ." George Bush, *Decision Points*.

161 "He would 'face serious consequences.'" George Bush, *Decision Points*.

162 "Hans Blix . . . called it 'rich in volume but poor in information.'" George Bush, *Decision Points*.

162 "I'd been receiving intelligence briefings . . ." George Bush, *Decision Points*.

162 "The conclusion that Saddam . . ." George Bush, *Decision Points*.

162 "In retrospect, of course, we all should've pushed harder . . ." George Bush, *Decision Points*.

171 "France had significant economic interest." George Bush, *Decision Points*.

171 "Hard to think of anything more insulting . . ." George Bush, *Decision Points*.

173 "There was some ambiguity in the international . . ." George Bush, *Decision Points*.

173 "We were going after al Qaeda at large." George Bush, *Decision Points*.

174 "The only logical conclusion was that he . . ." George Bush, *Decision Points*.

174 "I knew the consequences my order would . . ." George Bush, *Decision Points*.

175 "a sworn enemy of America . . ." George Bush, *Decision Points*.

175 "I knew the consequences my order would . . ." George Bush, *Decision Points.*

176 "Tony Blair and I agreed . . ." George Bush, *Decision Points.*

176 "We had ample justification to enforce . . ." George Bush, *Decision Points.*

178 "had discovered warheads that Saddam had failed . . ." George Bush, *Decision Points.*

181 "The overthrow of the regime that . . ." Allawi, *The Occupation of Iraq.*

191 "I didn't need to ask their opinion." George Bush, *Decision Points.*

192 "I knew where Colin Powell stood." George Bush, *Decision Points.*

192 "That was a massive blow to our credibility . . ." George Bush, *Decision Points.*

192 "No one was more shocked or angry . . ." George Bush, *Decision Points.*

193 "What's the difference?" George W. Bush, interview by Diane Sawyer, *Primetime*, ABC, December 16, 2003, transcript, http://abcnews.go.com/Primetime/story?id=131913&page=1.

199 "The nature of history is that . . ." George Bush, *Decision Points.*

206 "Over the years I've spent a great deal of time . . ." George Bush, *Decision Points.*

Additionally, the activities of the president of the United States and other public figures are well covered and documented by many news and information outlets. The actual recordings and writings of and by these public figures are a matter of public record and thus available for public examination and use.

The inevitable fact about this fictional story is that nobody knows whether it will become reality. Admittedly, it is probably a long shot, but if one knew how much longer George W. Bush will live, who will be elected president of the United States during the remainder of his life, if the Democrats or Republicans will control the US Congress, if the United States will rejoin the International Criminal Court, or who will be the ICC chief prosecutor during the remaining years of Mr. Bush's life—then he or she would be entitled to an opinion.

Acknowledgments

I would like to express much appreciation to a number of people who helped inform and guide this narrative. Much appreciation goes to William Schabas for making the Mount Everest of international law seem climbable. I thank my international criminal law experts in both Europe and the United States for their patient, educational, and useful assistance. If ever I took a course in international criminal law, Mike Kelly would be the person I would most like to have as my professor.

I thank my wonderful collection of editors, copyeditors, and assistants for their able and helpful assistance. If this book is any good, it is due in large part to their valuable, insightful, intelligent, and patient contributions.

I thank my longtime friend and attorney, Barry Hirsch, who never wavered in his belief and support.

Last but certainly not least, I thank my wife for a million reasons and counting, starting with saying yes to the most important question I ever asked.

About the Author

Terry Jastrow is a descendant of one of the pilgrims who arrived on the *Mayflower* and of American president John Adams. He was born in Colorado, grew up in Texas, and has lived his entire adult life in New York and California.

After graduating from college in 1970, Jastrow was hired by ABC Sports, and in December 1972, at age twenty-four, he became the youngest network television producer in history. He directed his first telecast in April 1974 and continued producing and directing at ABC Sports for twenty-two years. Jastrow was a producer/director of six Olympic Games, including the Summer Olympics in Los Angeles, where he directed the Opening and Closing Ceremonies. He was a director of Super Bowl XIX and produced or directed sixty major golf championships and approximately fifty episodes of ABC's *Wide World of Sports*. For his work in sports television, Jastrow won seven Emmy Awards (with seventeen nominations).

Next, he served as president of Jack Nicklaus Productions for twelve years. The company's principal business was to create and televise entertaining events that ultimately generated over fifty million dollars for worthy charities.

Later, Jastrow studied acting at the Lee Strasberg Theatre & Film Institute in New York City, where he was invited to be in Mr. Strasberg's Master Class. This led to an eventful few years as an actor, during which he did his share of theater, film, and television.

In 2015, Jastrow wrote, produced, and directed the feature film *The Squeeze*, which was released theatrically around the world and purchased by the Golf Channel for television.

In 2016, he wrote a stage play, *The Trial of Jane Fonda*, which was produced at the Park Theatre in London and received a nomination for Best New Play (off West End).

The Trial of Prisoner 043 is his first novel.

You can reach Terry at
Website: http://www.terryjastrow.com
Facebook: http://bit.ly/2rMNMQT
Twitter: @JastrowTerry
LinkedIn: http://bit.ly/2qUsBga